D1642332
THIS BOOK BELONGS TO

So Tom went down; and all the while he never saw the Irishwoman behind him (page 44)

One night, Tom crept away among the rocks and got to the cabinet (page 170)

THE WATER BABIES

THE WATER BABIES

by Charles Kingsley

NEW
ORCHARD

First published in 1990 by New Orchard Editions
Artillery House, Artillery Row, London SW1P 1RT, England

A Cassell imprint

ISBN 1-8507-9146-5

Typeset by Litho Link Ltd, Welshpool, Wales
Printed and bound in Norway

CONTENTS

LIST OF ILLUSTRATIONS

CHAPTER ONE

THE POOR LITTLE CHIMNEY SWEEP

nce upon a time there was a little chimney sweep, and his name was Tom. He lived in a great town in the north country, where there were plenty of chimneys to sweep, and plenty of money for Tom to earn and his master to spend.

He could not read or write, and did not care to do either; and he never washed himself, for there was no water in the court where he lived. He had never been taught to say his prayers. He had never heard of God, or of Christ, except in words which you never have heard, and which it would have been well if he had never heard.

Tom cried half his time, and laughed the other half. He cried when he had to climb the dark flues, rubbing his poor knees and elbows raw; and when the soot got into his eyes, which it did every day in the week; and when his master beat him, which he did every day in the week; and when he had not enough to eat, which happened every day in the week likewise. And he laughed the other half of the day, when he was tossing halfpennies with the other boys, or playing leap-frog over the posts, or bowling stones at the horses' legs as they trotted by, which last was excellent fun, when there was a wall at hand behind which to hide.

As for chimney sweeping, and being hungry, and being beaten, he took all that for the way of the world, like the rain and snow and thunder, and stood manfully with his back to it till it was over, as his old donkey did to a hailstorm, and then shook his ears and was as jolly as ever. Tom thought of the fine times coming, when he would be a man, and a master sweep, and sit in the public house with a quart of beer and a long pipe, and play cards for silver money, and wear velveteens, and keep a white bulldog with one black ear, and carry her puppies in his pocket, just like a man.

He would have apprentices, one, two, three, if he could. How he would bully them, and knock them about, just as his master did to him; and make them carry home the soot sacks, while he rode before them on his donkey, with a pipe in his mouth and a flower in his buttonhole, like a king at the head of his army.

Yes, there were good times coming; and, when his master let him have a pull at the leavings of his beer, Tom was the jolliest boy in the whole town.

One day a smart little groom rode into the court where Tom lived and halloed to him to ask where Mr. Grimes, the chimneysweep, lived. Now, Mr. Grimes was Tom's own master, and Tom was a good man of business, so he took the message. Mr. Grimes was to come up next morning to Sir John Harthover's, at the Place.

Now, I daresay, you never got up at three o'clock on a midsummer morning. I assure you that three o'clock on a midsummer morning is the pleasantest time of all the twenty-four hours, and all the three hundred and sixty-five days; and why everyone does not get up then, I never could tell, save that they are all determined to spoil their nerves and their complexions by doing all night what they might just as well do all day. But Tom, instead of going out to dinner at half-past eight at night, and to a ball at ten, and finishing off somewhere between twelve and four, went to bed at seven, when his master went to the public house, and slept like a dead pig, for which reason he was as pert as a gamecock (who always gets up early to wake the maids), and just ready to get up when the fine gentlemen and ladies were ready to go to bed. Tom loved that early part of the day.

So he and his master set out; Grimes rode the donkey in front, and Tom and the brushes walked behind; out of the court, and up the street, past the closed window shutters, and the winking, weary policeman, and the roofs all shining damply in the dull dawn.

They passed through the pitmen's village, all shut up and silent now, and through the turnpike; and then they were out in the real country and plodding along the black dusty road between black slag walls, with no sound but the groaning and thumping of the pit engine in the next field. But soon the road grew white, and the walls likewise; and at the wall's foot grew long grass and gay flowers, all drenched with dew; and instead of the groaning of the pit engine, they heard the skylark saying matins high up in the air, and the pit bird warbling in the sedges, as he had warbled all night long.

All else was silent. For old Mrs. Earth was still fast asleep, and like many pretty people, she looked still prettier asleep than awake.

The great elm trees in the gold-green meadows were fast asleep above, and the cows fast asleep beneath them; nay, the few clouds which were about were fast asleep likewise, and so tired that they had lain down on the earth to rest, in long white flakes and bars, among the stems of the elm trees, and along the tops of the alders by the silvery stream, waiting for the sun to bid them rise and go about their day's business in the vast ocean of clear blue overhead.

On they went; and Tom looked, and looked, for he never had been so far into the country before; and longed to get over a gate, and pick buttercups, and look for birds' nests in the hedge; but Mr. Grimes was a man of business, and would not have heard of that.

Soon they overtook a poor Irishwoman, trudging along with a bundle at her back. She had a dark shawl over her head, and a crimson madder petticoat, so you may be sure she came from Galway. She had neither shoes nor stockings, and limped along as if she were tired and footsore; but she was a very tall, handsome woman, with bright eyes and heavy black hair hanging around her cheeks. And she took Mr. Grimes' fancy so much, that when he came alongside he called out to her:

"This is a hard road for a dainty foot like that. Will ye up, lass, and ride behind me?"

But perhaps she did not admire Mr. Grimes' look and voice, for she answered quietly:

"No, thank you; I'd sooner walk with your little lad here."

"You may please yourself," growled Grimes, and went on smoking.

So she walked beside Tom and talked to him, and asked him where he lived and what he knew, and all about himself, till Tom thought he had never met such a pleasant-spoken woman. And she asked him, at last, whether he said his prayers, and seemed sad when he told her that he knew no prayers to say.

Then he asked her where she lived, and she said far away by the sea. And Tom asked her about the sea, and she told him how it rolled and roared over the rocks in winter nights, and lay still in the bright summer days for the children to bathe and play in it; and many a story more, till Tom longed to go and see the sea and bathe in it likewise.

At last, at the bottom of a hill, they came to a spring, not such a spring as you see here, which soaks up out of white gravel in the bog, among red flycatchers and pink bottle heath and sweet white orchids; nor such a one as you may see which bubbles up under the warm sandbank in the hollow lane by the great tuft of ladyferns, and makes the sand dance reels at the bottom, day and night, all the year round; not such a spring as either of those, but a real north country limestone fountain, like one of those in Sicily or Greece, where the people fancied that the nymphs sat cooling themselves on hot summer days, while the shepherds peeped at them from behind the bushes.

Out of a low cave of rock, at the foot of a limestone crag, the great fountain rose, leaping, and bubbling, and gurgling, so clear that you could not tell where the water ended and the air began; and ran away under the road, among blue geranium, and golden globeflower, and wild raspberry and the bird cherry with its tassels of snow; a stream large enough to turn a mill.

And there Grimes stopped and looked; and Tom looked too. Tom was wondering whether anything lived in that dark cave and came out at night to fly in the meadows. But Grimes was not wondering at all. Without a word, he got off his donkey and clambered over the low road wall and knelt down, and then began dipping his ugly head into the spring. And very dirty he made it.

Tom was picking the flowers as fast as he could. The Irishwoman helped him, and showed him how to tie them up; and a very pretty nosegay they had made between them. But when he saw Grimes actually wash, he stopped, quite astonished; and when Grimes had finished and began shaking his ears to dry them, he said:

"Why, master, I never saw you do that before."

"Nor will again, most likely. 'Twasn't for cleanliness I did it, but for coolness. I'd be ashamed to want washing every week or so, like any smutty collier lad."

"I wish I might go and dip my head in," said poor little Tom. "It must be as good as putting it under the town pump; and there is no guard here to drive a chap away."

"Thou come along," said Grimes; "what dost want with washing thyself? Thou did not drink half a gallon of beer last night, like me."

"I don't care what you say," said naughty Tom, and ran down to the stream and began washing his face.

Grimes was very sulky because the woman preferred Tom's company to his; so he dashed to him with horrid words, and dragged him up from his knees and began beating him. But Tom was accustomed to that, and got his head safe between Mr. Grimes' legs, and kicked his shins with all his might.

"Are you not ashamed of yourself, Thomas Grimes?" cried the Irishwoman over the wall.

Grimes looked up, startled at her knowing his name; but all he answered was, "No, nor never was yet," and went on beating Tom.

"True for you. If you ever had been ashamed of yourself, you would have gone over into Vendale long ago."

"What do you know about Vendale?" shouted Grimes; but he left off beating Tom.

"I know about Vendale, and about you too. I know, for instance, what happened in Aldermire Copse, by night, two years ago come Martinmas."

"You do?" shouted Grimes; and leaving Tom, he climbed up over the wall and faced the woman. Tom thought he was going to strike her; but she looked him too full and fierce in the face for that.

"Yes; I was there," said the Irishwoman quietly.

"You are no Irishwoman by your speech," said Grimes after many bad words.

"Never mind who I am. I saw what I saw; and if you strike that boy again, I can tell what I know."

Grimes seemed quite cowed, and got on his donkey without another word.

"Stop!" said the Irishwoman. "I have one more word for you both, for you will both see me again before all is over. Those that wish to be clean, clean they will be; and those that wish to be foul, foul they will be. Remember."

And she turned away and went through a gate into

Grimes rode the donkey, and Tom walked behind with the brushes (page 13)

So she walked beside Tom, who thought he had never met such a pleasant-spoken woman (page 15)

the meadow. Grimes stood still a moment, like a man who had been stunned. Then he rushed after her, shouting, "You come back." But when he got into the meadow, the woman was not there.

Had she hidden away? There was no place to hide in. But Grimes looked around, and Tom also, for he was as puzzled as Grimes himself at her disappearing so suddenly; but look where they would, she was not there.

Grimes came back again, as silent as a post, for he was a little frightened; and, getting on his donkey, filled a fresh pipe and smoked away, leaving Tom in peace.

And now they had gone three miles and more, and came to Sir John's lodge gates.

Grimes rang at the gate and out came a keeper on the spot to open it.

"I was told to expect thee," he said. "Now thou'lt be so good as to keep to the main avenue, and not let me find a hare or a rabbit on thee when thou comest back. I shall look sharp for one, I tell thee."

"Not if it's in the bottom of the soot bag," quoth Grimes, and at that he laughed; and the keeper laughed and said:

"If that's thy sort, I may as well walk up with thee to the hall."

"I think thou best had. It's thy business to see after thy game, man, and not mine."

So the keeper went with them; and to Tom's surprise, he and Grimes chatted together all the way quite pleasantly. He did not know that a keeper is only a poacher turned outside in, and a poacher a keeper turned inside out.

They walked up a great lime tree avenue, a full mile long, and between their stems Tom peeped trembling at the horns of the sleeping deer, which stood up among the ferns. Tom had never seen such enormous trees, and as he looked up he fancied that the blue sky rested on their heads. But he was puzzled very much by the strange murmuring noise, which followed them all the way. He was so much puzzled that at last he took courage to ask the keeper what it was.

He spoke very civilly, and called him Sir, for he was horribly afraid of him, which pleased the keeper, and he told him that they were the bees buzzing round the lime flowers.

"What are bees?" asked Tom.

"What make honey."

"What is honey?" asked Tom.

"Thou hold thy noise," said Grimes.

"Let the boy be," said the keeper. "He's a civil

young chap now, and that's more than he'll be long if he bides with thee."

Grimes laughed, for he took that for a compliment.

"I wish I were a keeper," said Tom, "to live in such a beautiful place, and wear green velveteens, and have a real dog whistle at my button, like you."

The keeper laughed; he was a kind-hearted enough fellow.

"Leave things as they are, lad. Thy life's safer than mine at all events. Isn't that so, Grimes?"

And Grimes laughed again, and then the two men began talking about some poaching fight.

And by this time they had arrived at the great iron gates in front of the house; and Tom stared through them at the rhododendrons and azaleas, which were all in flower; and then at the house itself, and wondered how many chimneys there were in it, and how long ago it was built, and what was the man's name that built it, and whether he got much money for his job.

These last were very difficult questions to answer. For Harthover had been built at ninety different times, and in nineteen styles, and looked as if somebody had built a whole street of houses of every imaginable shape, and then stirred them together with a spoon.

For the attics were Anglo-Saxon.

The third floor Norman.

The second Cinque-cento.

The first floor Elizabethan.

The right wing pure Doric.

The centre Early English, with a huge portico copied from the Parthenon.

The left wing pure Bœotian, which the country folk admired most of all, because it was just like the new barracks in the town, only three times as big.

The grand staircase was copied from the Catacombs at Rome.

The back staircase was copied from the Taj Mahal at Agra. This was built by Sir John's great-great-great-uncle who, in Lord Clive's Indian Wars, won plenty of money, plenty of wounds, and no more taste than his betters.

The cellars were copied from the caves of Elephanta.

The offices from the Pavilion at Brighton.

And the rest from nothing in heaven or on earth or under the earth.

This made Harthover House a great puzzle to antiquarians, and thoroughly confusing to critics and architects and all persons who like meddling in other people's business, and spending others' money. So they were all bothering poor Sir John year after year, and trying to talk him into spending a hundred thousand pounds or so in building, to please them and not himself. But he always put them off, like the canny north countryman he was. One wanted him to build a Gothic house, but he said he was no Goth; and another to build in Elizabethan style, but he said he lived under good Queen Victoria, and not good Queen Bess; and another was bold enough to tell him that his house was ugly, but he said he lived inside it, and not outside; and another, that there was no unity in it, but he said that that was just why he liked the old place. For he liked to see how each Sir John, and Sir Hugh, and Sir Ralph, and Sir Randal before him had left his mark upon the place, each after his own taste; and he had no more notion of disturbing his ancestors' work than of disturbing their graves. For now the house looked like a real live house that had a history and had grown and grown as the world grew. He believed that it was only an upstart fellow who did not know who his own grandfather was who would change it for some spick-and-span new Gothic or Elizabethan thing, which looked as if it had been all spawned in a night as mushrooms are. From which you may gather (if you have wit enough) that Sir John was a very sound-headed, sound-hearted squire, and just the man to keep the countryside in order, show good sport with his hounds, and generally set a good example in the country where he lived.

But Tom and his master did not go in through the great iron gates as if they had been Dukes or Bishops, but round the back way, and a very long way round it was; and into a little back door, where the ash boy let them in, yawning horribly. Then in a passage the housekeeper met them in such a stylish chintz dressing gown that Tom mistook her for My Lady herself, and she gave Grimes solemn orders about, "You will take care of this and take care of that," as if he were going up the chimneys and not Tom. And Grimes listened, and said every now and then under his voice, "You'll mind that, you little beggar?" And Tom did mind, at least all that he could. And then the housekeeper turned them into a grand room, all covered up in sheets of brown paper, and bade them begin in a lofty and tremendous voice; and so, after a whimper or two, and a kick from his master, into the grate Tom went, and up the chimney, while a house maid stayed in the room to watch the furniture. To her Mr. Grimes paid many playful and chivalrous compliments, but met with very slight encouragement in return.

How many chimneys Tom swept I cannot say, but he swept so many that he got very tired. He was puzzled too, for they were not like the town flues to which he was accustomed, but such as you would find (if you would only get up them and look, which, perhaps, you would not like to do) in old country houses: large and crooked chimneys, which had been altered again and again till they ran one into another like veins in a leaf. So Tom fairly lost his way in them; not that he much minded that, for even though he was in pitchy darkness, he was as much at home in a chimney as a mole is underground. At last, coming down what he thought was the right chimney, he came down the wrong one and found himself standing on the hearthrug in a room the like of which he had never seen before.

Tom stared around him. He had never been in gentlefolk's rooms except when the carpets were all up and the curtains down, and the furniture huddled together under a cover, and the pictures covered with cloths and dusters; and he had often enough wondered what the rooms were like when they were all ready for people of means to use. And now he saw, and he thought the sight very pretty.

The room was all dressed in white: white curtains, white bed spread, white furniture, and white walls, with just a few lines of pink here and there. The carpet had bright little flowers all over, and the walls amused Tom very much. There were pictures of ladies and gentlemen, and pictures of horses and dogs. The horses he liked, but he did not care much for the dogs because there were no bulldogs or even terriers among them.

There were two pictures on the walls which took his fancy most, and they did not feature animals at all. One was of a man in long garments with little children and their mothers round him, and he was laying his hand upon the children's heads. That was a very pretty picture, Tom thought, to hang in a lady's room. For he could see that it was a lady's room by the dresses he could see there.

The other picture was that of a man nailed to a cross, which greatly surprised Tom. He thought that he had seen nothing like it in a shop window. But why was it there? "Poor man," thought Tom, "and he looks so kind and quiet. But why should the lady have such a sad picture as that in her room? Perhaps it was some kinsman of hers, who had been killed in some terrible war far away, in foreign parts and she kept it there for a remembrance." And Tom felt sad, and awed, and he turned round to look at something else.

The next thing he saw, and that also puzzled him, was a washing stand with ewers and basins, and soap and brushes, and towels, and a large bath full of clean water. What a heap of things for washing! "She must be a very dirty lady," thought Tom, "by my master's rule, to want as much scrubbing as all that. But she must be very cunning to put the dirt out of the way so well afterwards, for I don't see a speck in the room, not even on the towels."

And then, looking at the bed, he saw that "dirty lady" and held his breath with astonishment.

Under the snow-white coverlet, upon the snow-white pillow, lay the most beautiful little girl that Tom had ever seen. Her cheeks were almost as white as the pillow, and her hair was like threads of gold spread over the bed. She might have been as old as Tom or maybe a year or two older; but Tom did not think of that. He thought only of her delicate skin and golden hair, and wondered whether she was a real live person or one of the wax dolls he had seen in the shops. But when he saw her breathe, he made up his mind that she was alive, and stood staring at her as if she had been an angel out of heaven.

No. She cannot be dirty. She never could have been dirty, thought Tom to himself. And then he thought, "And are all people like that when they are washed?" And he looked at his own wrist, and tried to rub the soot off, and wondered whether it ever would come off. "Certainly I should look much prettier clean, if I became at all like her."

And looking round he suddenly saw, standing close to him, a little, ugly, blackened, ragged figure, with bleared eyes. He turned on it angrily. What did such a little animal-like creature want in that sweet young lady's room? And behold, it was himself, reflected in a great mirror, another thing the like of which Tom had never seen before.

And Tom, for the first time in his life, found out that he was dirty. He burst into tears with shame and anger and turned to sneak up the chimney again and hide; and he upset the fender and threw the fire irons down with a noise like ten thousand tin kettles tied to ten thousand mad dogs' tails.

Up jumped the little girl, and, seeing Tom, screamed as shrill as any peacock. In rushed a stout old nurse from the next room, and seeing Tom likewise, made up her mind that he had come to rob, plunder, destroy and burn. She sprang at him as he lay where he had fallen over the fender, so fast that she caught him by the jacket.

But she did not hold him. Tom had been in a policeman's hands many a time, and, what is more out of them too. And he would have been ashamed ever to face his friends again if he had been stupid enough to be caught by an old woman. So he slipped under the good lady's arm, across the room, and out of the window in a moment.

He did not need to drop out, though he would have done so bravely enough, nor even to let himself down a spout, which would have been an old game to him. For once he had climbed up a spout to the church roof to take jackdaw's eggs, he said; but the policemen said to steal lead; and when he was seen on high, he sat there till the sun got too hot, and came down by another spout, leaving the policemen to go back to the stationhouse and begin to eat their dinners.

But all under the window spread a tree, with large leaves and sweet white flowers almost as big as his head. It was magnolia, I suppose; but Tom knew nothing about that and cared less. Down the tree he went like a cat, and across the garden lawn, and over the iron railings, and up the park to the forest, leaving the old nurse to scream murder and fire at the window.

The undergardener, who was mowing, saw Tom, threw down his scythe, caught his leg in it, and cut his shin open (and later had to stay in bed a week), but in his hurry he didn't notice and gave chase to poor Tom. The dairymaid heard the noise, got the churn between her knees and tumbled over it, spilling all the cream; and yet she jumped up and gave chase to Tom.

A groom, cleaning Sir John's horse in the stables, let him loose, whereby he kicked himself lame in five minutes, but the groom also gave chase to Tom. Grimes upset the soot sack in the new-laid gravel of the yard, and spoiled it all utterly; but he ran out and gave chase to Tom. The old steward opened the park gate in such a hurry that he caught his pony's chin upon the spikes, and, for all I know, it hangs there still; but he left the pony, and gave chase to Tom. The ploughman left his horses at the headland, and one jumped over the fence, and pulled the other into the ditch, plough and all; but this man too gave chase to Tom.

The keeper, who was taking a stoat out of a trap, let the stoat go and caught his own finger; but he jumped up and ran after Tom, and, considering what he said and how he looked, I should have been sorry for Tom if he had caught him.

Sir John looked out of his study window (for he was up early in the morning), and up at the nurse, and a martin dropped mud in his eye so that he had to send for the doctor later on; and yet he ran out and gave chase to Tom. The Irishwoman was just then walking up to the house to beg (she must have reached the place by some byway) but she threw away her bundle and gave chase to Tom with the rest. Only my Lady did not give chase, for when she had put her head out of the window, her night wig fell into the garden, and she had to ring for her lady's maid and send her down to collect it privately, which put her completely out of the running. So she came in nowhere, and is consequently not placed in this particular race.

In a word, never was there heard at Hall Place (not even when the fox was killed in the conservatory among acres of broken glass and tons of smashed flower pots) such a noise, row, hubbub, babel, shindy, hullabaloo, stramash, charivari, and total contempt of dignity, repose, and order, as that day when Grimes, the gardener, the groom, the dairy-maid, Sir John, the steward, the ploughman, the keeper, and the Irishwoman all ran through the park, shouting, "Stop thief!" in the belief that Tom had at least a thousand pounds' worth of jewels in his empty pockets; and even the magpies and jays followed Tom, screaking and screaming as if he were a hunted fox, beginning to droop his brush in tiredness.

And all the while poor Tom sped through the park on his little bare feet, like a small frightened animal fleeing to the forest. Alas for him! There was no father animal ready to take his part.

However, Tom did not remember ever having a father; so he did not look for one, and expected to have to take care of himself. As for running, he could keep up with any stagecoach for a couple of miles if he had a bet on. Therefore his pursuers found it very difficult to catch him, and we will hope that they did not catch him at all.

Tom, of course, made for the woods. He had never been in a forest in his life, but he was sharp enough to know that he might hide in a bush or swarm up a tree and have hope of saving himself more there than in the open. If he had not known that, he would have been more foolish than a mouse or a minnow.

But when he got into the woods, he found it a very different sort of place from what he had imagined. He pushed into a thick cover of rhododendrons and at once found himself caught in a trap. The boughs laid hold of his legs and arms, poked him in his face and his stomach, made him shut his eyes tight (though that was no great loss, for he could not see at best a yard before his nose); and when he got through the rhododendrons, the hassock grass and sedges tumbled him over, and cut his poor little fingers most spitefully as he fell; the birches birched him as soundly as if he had been a naughty schoolboy at Eton, and over the face too (which is not a fair beating, as all brave boys will agree), and the lawyer vines tripped him up, and tore his shins as if they had sharks' teeth, which lawyers are likely enough to have.

"I must get out of this," thought Tom.

But how to get out was the big problem. And, indeed, I don't think he would ever have done so at all, but have stayed there till the cockrobins covered him with leaves, like they did in the fairy story about the babes in the woods when the poor babes died, if he had not suddenly run his head against a wall.

Now, running your head against a wall is not pleasant, especially if it is a loose wall, with the stones all set on edge, and a sharp-cornered one hits you between the eyes and makes you see all manner of beautiful stars. The stars are very beautiful, certainly, but unfortunately they go in the twenty-thousandth part of a split second, and the pain which comes after them does not. And so Tom hurt his head; but he was a brave boy, and did not mind that a penny. He guessed that over the wall was his escape, and up it he went, and over like a squirrel.

And there he was, out on the great grouse moors which the country folk called Harthover Fell, heather and bog and rock stretching away and up, up to the very sky.

Now, Tom was a cunning little fellow, as cunning as an old stag. Why not? Though he was but ten years old, he had lived longer than most stags, and had more wits to start with into the bargain.

He knew as well as a stag that if he doubled back he might throw the hounds off. So the first thing he did when he was over the wall was to make the neatest double sharp to his right, and run along under the wall for nearly half a mile.

So Sir John, and the keeper, and the steward, and the gardener, and the ploughman, and the dairy-maid, and all the hue-and-cry together, went that half a mile in the very opposite direction, and inside the wall, leaving him a mile off on the outside. Tom heard their shouts die away in the woods and chuckled to himself merrily.

At last he came to a dip in the land and went to the bottom of it, and then he turned bravely away from the wall and across the moor; for he knew that he had put a hill between him and his pursuers, and could go on without their seeing him.

But the Irishwoman, alone of them all, had seen which way Tom went. She had kept ahead of everyone the whole time; and yet she neither walked

Under the snow white coverlet, lay the most beautiful little girl that Tom had ever seen (page 29)

The dairymaid caught the churn between her knees, but jumped up and gave chase too (page 31)

nor ran. She went along quite smoothly and gracefully, while her feet twinkled past each other so fast that you could not see which was in the front. Everyone asked the other who the strange woman was, and all agreed, for want of anything better to say, that she must be in league with Tom.

But when she came to the forest they lost sight of her; and they couldn't help it. For she went quietly over the wall after Tom and followed him wherever he went. Sir John and the rest saw no more of her; and out of sight was out of mind.

And now Tom was well away into the heather, over just such a moor as those which you have read about, except that there were rocks and stones lying about everywhere, and that, instead of the moor growing flat as he went up, it grew more and more broken and hilly. However, it was not so rough that it kept little Tom from jogging along well enough, and he found time too to stare at the strange place, which was like a new world to him.

So Tom went on and on, he hardly knew why, but he liked the great, wide, strange place and the cool, fresh, bracing air. But he went more and more slowly as he got higher up the hill, for now the ground grew very bad indeed. Instead of soft turf and springy heather, he met great patches of flat limestone rock, just like badly made pavements, with deep cracks between the stones and ledges filled with ferns; so he had to hop from stone to stone, and now and then he slipped in between and hurt his little bare toes, though they were tolerably tough ones; but still he continued on and up, he could not tell why.

What would Tom have said if he had seen, walking over the moor behind him, the very same Irishwoman who had taken his part on the road? But whether it was that he did not often look behind him, or whether it was that she kept out of sight behind the rocks and knolls, he never saw her, though she saw him.

And now he began to get a little hungry and very thirsty, for he had run a long way and the sun had risen high in heaven, and the rock was as hot as an oven, and the air danced reels over it, as it does over a limekiln, till everything round seemed quivering and melting in the glare.

But he could see nothing to eat or drink at all.

The heath was full of bilberries and whinberries, but they had no fruit yet for it was June. And as for water, who can find that on top of a limestone rock? Now and then he passed by a deep, dark sinkhole going down into the earth, as if it were the chimney of some dwarf's house underground; and more than once, as he passed, he could hear water falling, trickling, and tinkling many, many feet below. How he longed to get down to it, and have a drink, and cool his poor, baked lips! But, brave little chimney sweep that he was, he dared not climb down such chimneys as those.

So he went on and on, till his head was spinning with the heat, and he thought he heard church bells ringing a long way off.

"Ah!" he thought, "where there is a church there will be houses and people; and, perhaps, someone will give me a bite to eat." So he went that way to look for the church, for he was sure that he heard the bells quite plain.

And in a minute more, when he looked round, he stopped again and said, "Why, what a big place the world is!"

And so it was; for, from the top of the mountain he could see – what could he not see?

Behind him, far below, was Harthover and the dark woods and the shining salmon river; and on his left, far below, was the town and the smoking chimneys of the collieries; and far, far away, the river widened to the shining sea, and little white specks, which were ships, lay on its bosom. Before him, spread out like a map, lay great plains and farms and villages, amid dark knots of trees. They all seemed at his very feet, but he had the sense to see that they were long miles away.

And to his right rose moor after moor, hill after hill, till they faded away, blue into blue sky. But between him and those moors, and really at his very feet, lay something to which, as soon as Tom saw it, he determined to go, for that was the special place for him.

It was a deep, deep green and rocky valley, very narrow and filled with woods; but through these, hundreds of feet below him, he could see a clear stream. Oh, if he could but get down to that stream! Then, by the stream, he saw the roof of a little cottage and a little garden set out in squares and beds. And there was a tiny little red thing moving in the garden, no bigger than a fly. As Tom looked down, he saw that it was a woman in a red petticoat. Ah! perhaps she would give him something to eat. He certainly felt in need of nourishment. And there were the church bells ringing again. Surely there must be a village down there. Well, nobody would know him or what had happened at the Place. The news could not have reached there yet, even if Sir John had set all the policemen in the country after him. And he could get down there in five minutes.

Tom was quite right about the hue-and-cry not having got so far, for, without knowing it, he had come the best part of ten miles from Harthover. But he was wrong about getting down in five minutes, for the cottage was more than a mile off, and a good thousand feet below.

However, down he went like the brave little man he was, though he was very footsore, and tired, and hungry, and thirsty. The churchbells rang so loud that he began to think they must be inside his own head, and the river chimed and tinkled far below; and this was the song which it sang:

Clear and cool, clear and cool,
By laughing shallow and dreaming pool;
Cool and clear, cool and clear
By shining shingle and foaming wear;
Under the crag where the ouzel sings,
And the ivied wall where the churchbell rings,
Undefiled, for the undefiled;
Play by me, bathe in me, mother and child.

Dank and foul, dank and foul,
By the smoky town in its murky cowl;
Foul and dank, foul and dank,
By wharf and sewer and slimy bank;

Darker and darker the farther I go,
Baser and baser the richer I grow;
Who dare sport with the sin-defiled?
Shrink from me, turn from me, mother and child.

Strong and free, strong and free,
The floodgates are open, away to the sea,
Free and strong, free and strong,
Cleansing my streams as I hurry along,
To the golden sands, and the leaping bar,
And the taintless tide that awaits me afar.
As I lose myself in the infinite main,
Like a soul that has sinned and is pardoned again.
Undefiled, for the undefiled;
Play by me, bathe by me, mother and child.

So Tom went down; and all the while he never knew that the Irishwoman was following behind him.

CHAPTER TWO

TOM BECOMES A WATER-BABY

mile off and a thousand feet down. That's how far Tom went, though it seemed as if he could have chucked a pebble onto the back of the woman in the red petticoat who was weeding in the garden, or even across the dale to the rocks beyond. For the bottom of the valley was just one field broad, and on the other side ran the stream; and above it, dun crag, dun down, dun stair, dun moor walled up to heaven.

A quiet, silent, rich, happy place; a narrow crack cut deep into the earth, deep and out of the way. The name of the place is Vendale, and if you want to see it for yourself, you must go up into the High Craven and search from Bolland Forest north by Ingleborough, to the Nine Standards and Cross Fell; and if you have not found it, you must turn south and search the Lake Mountains down to Scaw Fell and the sea; and then, if you have not found it, you must go northward again by merry Carlisle, and search the Cheviots all across from Annan Water to Berwick Law.

So Tom started down, and first he went down three hundred feet of steep heather mixed with loose brown gritstone, as rough as a file. This was not pleasant to his poor little heels as he came bump, stump, jump, down the hill. And still he thought he could throw a stone into the garden.

Then he went down three hundred feet of limestone terraces, one below the other, as straight as if a carpenter had ruled them with a ruler and then cut them out with a chisel. There was no heath there, but:

First, a little grass slope, covered with the prettiest flowers, rockrose and saxifrage, and thyme and basil, and all sorts of sweet herbs.

Then bump down a two-foot step of limestone.

Then another bump bit of grass and flowers.

Then bump down a one-foot step.

Then another bit of grass and flowers for fifty yards, as steep as a house roof, where he had to slide down on his dear little tail.

Then another step of stone, ten feet high; and there he had to stop himself and crawl along the edge to find a crack, for if he had rolled over, he would have rolled right into the old woman's garden and frightened her out of her wits.

Then, when he had found a dark, narrow crack, full of green-stalked fern, such as hangs in the basket in the drawing room, and had crawled down through it with knees and elbows, as he would down a narrow chimney, there was another grass slope, and another step, and so on, till – oh, dear me! I wish it was all over; and so did he. And yet he thought he could throw a stone so it would land in the old woman's garden.

At last he came to a bank of beautiful shrubs, whitebeam with its great silver-backed leaves, and mountain ash, and oak; and below them cliff and crag, cliff and crag, with great beds of crown ferns and wood sedge; while through the shrubs he could see the stream sparkling, and hear it murmur on the white pebbles as though it was but a few steps away. He did not know that it was three hundred feet below.

You would have been giddy, perhaps, at looking down; but Tom was not. He was a brave little chimney sweep; and when he found himself on the top of a high cliff, instead of sitting down and crying for his mother (though he never had had any mother to cry for), he said, "Ah, this will just suit me!" And, though he was very tired, down he went by stock and stone, sedge and ledge, bush and rush, as if he had been born a jolly little monkey with four hands instead of two.

And all the while he never saw the Irishwoman coming down behind him.

But he was getting terribly tired now. The burning sun on the fells had eaten at his energy, but the damp heat of the woody crag took even more out of him. The perspiration ran out of the ends of his fingers and toes and washed him cleaner than he had been for a whole year. But, of course, he dirtied everything terribly as he went. There has been a great black smudge all down the crag ever since. And there have been more black beetles in Vendale since then than ever were known before; all, of course, owing to Tom's having blacked the original papa of them all, just as he was setting off to be married, with a sky blue coat and scarlet leggings, as smart as a gardener's dog with a fresh bunch of polyanthus in his mouth.

At last he got to the bottom. But, behold, it was not the bottom, as people usually find when they are coming down a mountain. For at the foot of the crag were heaps and heaps of fallen limestone of every size from that of your head to that of a stage coach, with holes between them full of sweet heath fern; and before Tom got through them, he was out in the bright sunshine again; and then he felt, once for all and suddenly, as people generally do, that he was b-e-a-t, beat.

He could not go on. The sun was burning, and yet he felt a chill all over. He was quite empty, and yet he felt quite sick. There were but two hundred yards of smooth pasture between him and the cottage, and yet he could not walk it. He could hear the stream murmur only one field beyond it, and yet it seemed to him to be a hundred miles off.

He lay down on the grass till the beetles ran over him and the flies settled on his nose. I don't know when he would have risen again if the gnats and the midges had not taken compassion on him. But the gnats blew their trumpets so loud in his ear, and the midges nibbled so eagerly at his hands and face wherever they could find a place free from soot, that at last he woke up and stumbled away, down over a low wall and into a narrow road, and up to the cottage door.

And a neat, pretty cottage it was, with clipped yew hedges all round the garden, and yews inside too, cut into peacocks and trumpets and teapots and all kinds of queer shapes. And out of the open door came a noise like that of the frogs on a huge pond when they know that it is going to be scorching hot tomorrow; and how they know that I don't know, and you don't know, and nobody knows.

He came slowly up to the open door, which was all hung round with clematis and roses, and then peeped in, half afraid.

And there by the empty fireplace, which was filled with a pot of sweet herbs, sat the nicest old woman that ever was seen, in her red petticoat and short dimity bedgown, and clean white cap with a black silk handkerchief over it, tied under her chin. At her feet sat the grandfather of all the cats; and opposite her, on two benches, sat twelve or fourteen neat, rosy, chubby little children, learning their ABCs; and gabble enough they made about it.

Such a pleasant cottage it was, with a shiny, clean, stone floor and curious old prints on the walls, and an old black oak sideboard full of bright pewter and brass dishes, and a cuckoo-clock in the corner, which began shouting as soon as Tom appeared: not that it was frightened of Tom, but that it was just eleven o'clock.

All the children started at Tom's dirty, blackened figure. The girls began to cry and the boys began to laugh, and all pointed at him rudely; but Tom was too tired to care about it.

"What art thou, and what dost thou want?" cried the old dame. "A chimney sweep! Away with thee! I'll have no sweeps here."

"Water," said poor little Tom, quite faint.

"Water? There's plenty i' the beck," she said, quite sharply.

"But I can't get there; I'm most dead with hunger and thirst." And Tom sank down upon the doorstep and laid his head against the post.

And the old dame looked at him through her spectacles one minute, and two, and three; and then she said, "He's sick; and a bairn's a bairn, sweep or none."

"Water," said Tom.

"God forgive me!" she said, taking off her spectacles; and she rose and came to Tom. "Water's bad for thee; I'll give thee milk." And she toddled off into the next room and brought a cup of milk and a bit of bread.

Tom drank the milk off at one gulp, and then looked up, revived.

"Where didst come from?" said the dame.

"Over Fell, there," said Tom, and pointed up into the sky.

"Over Harthover? and down Lewthwaite Crag? Art sure thou art not lying?"

"Why should I?" said Tom, and leaned his head against the post.

"And how got ye up there?"

"I came over from the Place." Then Tom was so tired and desperate he had no heart or time to think of a story, so he told all the truth in a few words.

"Bless thy little heart! And thou hast not been stealing, then?"

"No."

"Bless thy little heart! and I'll warrant not. Why, God's guided the bairn, because he was innocent! Away from the Place, and over Harthover Fell, and down Lewthwaite Crag! Who ever heard the like, if God hadn't led him? Why dost not eat thy bread?"

"I can't."

"It's good enough, for I made it myself."

"I can't," said Tom.

"Bless thy pretty heart! The bairn's sick. Come wi' me, an' I'll hap thee up somewhere. If thou wert a bit cleaner I'd put thee in my own bed, for the Lord's sake. But come along here."

But when Tom tried to get up, he was so tired and giddy that she had to help him and lead him so that he didn't fall down.

She put him in an outhouse upon soft sweet hay and an old rug, and bade him sleep off his walk, and she would come to him when school was over in an hour's time.

And so she went in again, expecting Tom to fall fast asleep at once.

But Tom did not fall asleep.

Instead, he turned and tossed and kicked about in the strangest way, and felt so hot all over that he longed to get into the river and cool himself; and then he fell half asleep, and dreamt that he heard the little girl crying to him, "Oh, you're so dirty; go and be washed;" and then he heard the Irishwoman saying, "Those that wish to be clean, clean they will be." And then he heard the church bells ring so loud and so close to him, that he was sure it must be Sunday, in spite of what the old dame had said; and he decided to go to church and see what a church was like inside, for he had never been in one, poor little fellow, in all his life. But he knew the people would never let him in, dirty as he was. He must go to the river and wash first. And he said out loud again and again, though being half asleep he did not know it, "I must be clean, I must be clean."

And all of a sudden he found himself, not in the outhouse on the hay, but in the middle of a meadow

There by the empty fireplace sat the nicest old woman that ever was seen (page 51)

They heard the whole story from Ellie, the little girl in white (page 61)

over the road, with the stream just before him, saying continually, "I must be clean, I must be clean." He had reached there on his own legs, between being asleep and awake, as children will often get out of bed and go about the room when they are not well. But he was not a bit surprised, and went on to the bank of the brook and lay down on the grass, and looked into the clear, clear, limestone water, with every pebble at the bottom bright and clean, while the little silver trout dashed about in fright at the sight of his dirty face; and he dipped his hand in and found it so cool, cool, cool; and he said, "I will be a fish. I will swim in the water. I must be clean, I must be clean."

So he pulled off all his clothes in such haste that he tore some of them, which was easy enough with such ragged old things. And he put his poor, hot, sore feet into the water, and then his legs; and the farther he went in, the more the churchbells began to ring in his head.

"Ah!" said Tom, "I must be quick and wash myself; the bells are ringing quite loud now; and they will stop soon, and then the door will be shut and I shall never be able to get in at all."

Tom was mistaken: for in England the church doors are left open all during the service for everybody who wants to come in. But Tom did not know that, any more than he knew many other things which people ought to know.

And all the while he never saw the Irishwoman, not behind him this time, but ahead.

For just before he came to the riverside, she had stepped down into the cool, clear water; and her shawl and her petticoat floated away, and the green waterweeds floated round her sides, and the white waterlilies floated round her head, and the fairies of the stream came up from the bottom and swam around her, and bore her away and down upon their arms. For she was the Queen of them all, and perhaps of more besides.

"Where have you been?" they asked her.

"I have been smoothing sick folk's pillows and whispering sweet dreams into their ears; opening cottage windows to let out the stifling air; coaxing little children away from gutters and foul pools where fever breeds; turning women from the tavern door, and staying men's hands as they were going to strike their wives; doing all that I can to help those who will not help themselves: and little enough that is, and weary work for me. But I have brought you a new little brother, and watched over him all the way here."

Then all the fairies laughed for joy at the thought that they had a little brother coming.

"But mind, maidens, he must not see you or know that you are here. He is but a ruffian now, and like the beasts which cannot think; and from the beasts such as these he must learn. So you must not play with him, or speak to him, or let him see you; but you must keep him from being harmed."

Then the fairies were sad because they could not play with their new brother, but they always did what they were told.

And their Queen floated away, down the river; and whither she went, thither she came. But all this Tom, of course, never saw or heard; and perhaps if he had it would have made little difference in the story, for he was so hot and thirsty, and longed so to be clean for once, that he tumbled himself as quick as he could into the clear, cool stream.

And he had not been in it two minutes before he fell fast asleep, into the quietest, sunniest, cosiest sleep that ever he had in his life; and he dreamed about the green meadows on which he had walked that morning, and the tall elm trees, and the sleeping cows; and after that he really dreamed of nothing at all.

The reason that he fell into such a delightful sleep

is very simple, and yet hardly any one has discovered it. It was merely that the fairies took him.

Some people think that there are no fairies. But it is a wide world, and plenty of room in it for fairies without people seeing them unless, of course, they look in the right place. The most wonderful and the strongest things in the world, you know, are just the things which no one can see. There is life in you, and it is the life in you which makes you grow, and move, and think; and yet you can't see it. And there is steam in a steam engine, and that is what makes it move; and yet you can't see it; and so there may be fairies in the world.

At all events, we will make believe that there are fairies in the world. It will not be the last time by many a one that we shall have to make believe. And yet, after all, there is no need for that. There must be fairies, for this is a fairy tale and how can one have a fairy tale if there are no fairies?

The kind old dame came back at twelve, when school was over, to look at Tom, but there was no Tom there. She looked for his footprints, but the ground was so hard that there was no slot, as they say in dear old North Devon.

So the old dame went in again quite sulky, thinking that little Tom had tricked her with a false story, and shammed illness, and then run away again.

But she altered her mind the next day. For, when Sir John and the rest of them had run themselves out of breath and lost Tom, they went home again, feeling very foolish.

And they looked more foolish still when Sir John heard more of the story from the nurse; and even more foolish still when he heard the whole story from Ellie, the little girl in white. All she had seen was a poor little chimney sweep, crying and sobbing, and about to go up the chimney again. Of course, she was very much frightened, and no wonder. But that was all. The boy had taken nothing in the room; by the marks of his little sooty feet, they could see that he had never been off the hearthrug till the nurse caught hold of him. It was all a mistake.

So Sir John told Grimes to go home and promised him five shillings if he would bring the boy quietly up to him, without beating him, that he might get at the truth. For he took for granted, and Grimes too, that Tom had made his way home.

But no Tom came back to Mr. Grimes that evening, and he went to the police to tell them to look out for the boy. But no Tom was heard of. As for his having gone over those great fells to Vendale, they no more dreamt of that than of his having gone to the moon.

So Mr. Grimes came up to Harthover next day with a very sour face, but when he got there, Sir John was over the hills and far away and Mr. Grimes had to sit in the outer servants' hall all day, and drink strong ale to wash away his sorrows; and they were washed away long before Sir John came back.

For good Sir John had slept very badly that night; and he said to his lady, "My dear, the boy must have got over into the grouse moors and lost himself; and he lies very heavily on my conscience, poor little lad. But I know what I will do."

So, at five the next morning up he got, and into his bath, and into his shooting jacket and gaiters, and into the stable yard, like a fine old English gentleman, with a face as red as a rose, and a hand as hard as a table, and a back as broad as a bullock's, and bade them bring his shooting pony, and the keeper to come on his pony, and the huntsman, and the first whip, and the second whip, and the under-keeper with the bloodhound on a leash, a great dog as tall as a calf, of the hue of a gravel walk, with mahogany ears and nose, and a throat like a churchbell. They took him up to the place where Tom had gone into the woods, and there the hound lifted up his mighty voice and told them all he knew.

Then he took them to the place where Tom had climbed the wall, and they shoved it down in order to get through.

And then the wise dog took them over the moor, and over the fells, step by step, very slowly; for the scent was a day old, you know, and very light from the heat and drought. But that was why cunning old Sir John started at five in the morning.

And at last the dog came to the top of Lewthwaite Crag, and there he bayed, and looked up in their faces as much as to say, "I tell you he went down here!"

They could hardly believe that Tom would have gone so far; and when they looked at that awful cliff, they could never believe that he would have dared to face it. But if the dog said so, it must be true.

"Heaven forgive us!" said Sir John. "If we find him at all, we shall find him lying at the bottom." And he slapped his great hand upon his great thigh and said in a loud voice:

"Who will go down over Lewthwaite Crag and see if that boy is alive? Oh, that I were twenty years younger, I would go down myself!" And so he would have done, as well as any sweep in the county. Then he said:

"Twenty pounds to the man who brings me that boy alive!" and, as was his way, what he said he meant.

Now among the lot was a little groom boy, a very little groom indeed, the same one who had ridden up the court and told Tom to come to the Hall; and he said:

"Twenty pounds or none, I will go down over Lewthwaite Crag if it's only for the poor boy's sake. For he was as well-spoken a little chap as ever climbed a flue."

So down over Lewthwaite Crag he went, a very smart groom at the top and a very shabby one at the bottom; for he tore his gaiters, and he tore his breeches, and he tore his jacket, and he burst his braces, and he burst his boots, and he lost his hat, and what was worst of all, he lost his shirt pin, which he prized very much, for it was gold, and he won it in a raffle at Malton, and there was a figure at the top of it of a noble old mare as natural as life, so it was a really severe loss; but he never saw anything of Tom.

And all the while Sir John and the rest were riding round, a full three miles to the right and back again, to get into Vendale and to the foot of the crag.

When they came to the old dame's school, all the children came out to look. And the old woman herself came out too; and when she saw Sir John, she curtsied very low, for she was a tenant of his.

"Well, dame, and how are you?" said Sir John.

"Blessings on you as broad as your back, Harthover," says she (she didn't call him Sir John, but only Harthover, for that is the fashion in the north country) "and welcome into Vendale; but you're no hunting the fox this time o' the year?"

"I am hunting, and strange game too," said he.

"Blessings on your heart, and what makes you look so sad the morn?"

"I'm looking for a lost child, a chimney sweep who has run away."

"Oh, Harthover, Harthover," says she, "ye were always a just and merciful man; and ye'll no harm the poor little lad if I give you tidings of him?"

"Not I, not I, dame. I'm afraid we chased him out of the house all on a miserable mistake, and the hound has traced him to the top of Lewthwaite Crag, and . . . "

Whereat the old dame broke out crying, without letting him finish his story.

"So he told me the truth after all, poor little dear! Ah, first thoughts are best, and a body's heart'll guide them right if they will but hearken to it." And then she told Sir John everything.

"Bring the dog here, and set him off," said Sir John, without another word, and he set his teeth very hard.

And the dog sped away at once, going round the back of the cottage, over the road and over the meadow, and through a bit of alder copse; and there, upon the stump of an alder tree, they saw Tom's clothes lying. And then they knew as much about it all as there was any need to know.

And Tom?

Ah, now comes the most wonderful part of this wonderful story. When Tom woke, for of course he woke (children always wake after they have slept exactly as long is good for them), he found himself swimming in the stream. He was about four inches long, or, that I may be accurate 3.87902 inches, and had round the parotid region of his fauces a set of external gills (I hope you understand all the big words) just like those of a water newt. These he mistook for a lace frill till he pulled at them, found he hurt himself, and made up his mind that they were a part of himself and best left alone.

In fact, the fairies had turned him into a water-baby.

A water-baby? You never heard of a water-baby? Perhaps not. That is the very reason why this story was written. There are a great many things in the world which you never heard of, and a great many things which nobody will ever hear of, at least until the coming of the Golden Age, when people shall be wiser than they are now.

"But there are no such things as water-babies."

How do you know that? Have you been there to see? And if you had been there to see, and had seen none, that would not prove that there were none. No one has a right to say that no water-babies exist, till they have seen no water-babies existing; which is quite a different thing, mind, from not seeing water-babies; and a thing which nobody ever did, or perhaps ever will, do.

"But surely if there were water-babies, somebody would once have caught one?"

Well. How do you know that somebody has not caught one?

No water-babies, indeed! Why, wise men of old said that everything on earth had its double in the water; and you may see that that is, if not quite true, still just as true as most other theories which you are likely to hear for many a day. There are land-babies. Then why not water-babies? Are there not water-rats, water-flies, water-crickets, water-crabs, water-tortoises, water-scorpions, water-tigers and water-hogs, water-cats and water dogs; sea-lions and sea-bears, sea-horses and sea-elephants, sea-mice and sea-urchins, sea razors and sea-pens, sea-combs and sea-fans; and of plants, are there not water-grass, and water-crowfoot, water-milfoil, and so on without end?

"But all these things are only nicknames; the water things are not really akin to the land things."

That's not always true. They are, in millions of cases, not only of the same family, but actually the same individual creatures. Do not even you know that a green drake, and an alder fly and a dragonfly, live under water till they change their skins, just as Tom changed his? And if a water animal can continually change into a land animal, why should not a land animal sometimes change into a water animal?

If people say that, if there are water-babies they must grow into water-men and women, ask them how they know that they do not?

Am I in earnest? Oh, dear no! Don't you know that this is a fairy tale, and all fun and fantasy; and that you are not to believe one word of it, even if it is actually true?

But at all events, it happened to Tom. And, therefore, the keeper, and the groom, and Sir John made a great mistake, and were very unhappy (Sir John, at least) without any reason, when they found a black thing in the water, and said it was Tom's body and that he had been drowned. They were utterly mistaken. Tom was quite alive, and cleaner and merrier than he ever had been.

The fairies had washed him, you see, in the swift river, so thoroughly, that not only his dirt, but his whole husk and shell had been washed off, and the pretty little real Tom was washed out of the inside of it and swam away, as a caddis does when its case of stones and silk is bored through, and away it goes on its back, paddling to the shore, there to split its skin, and fly away as a caddis fly, on four fawn wings, with long legs and horns. They are foolish fellows, the caddis flies, and throw themselves into the candle at night if you leave the door open. We hope Tom will be wiser, now that he is safely out of his sooty old shell.

But good Sir John did not understand all this, not knowing anything about zoology, and he took it into his head that Tom had drowned. When they looked into the empty pockets of his shell and found no jewels or money there, nothing but three marbles and a brass button with a string attached to it, then Sir John did something near to crying as ever he did in his life, and blamed himself more bitterly than he need have done.

So he snuffled, and the groom boy cried, and the huntsman cried, and the dame cried, and the little girl cried, and the dairymaid cried, and the old nurse cried (for it was somewhat her fault), and my lady cried, for though people have wigs, that is no reason why they should not have hearts. But Grimes did not cry, for Sir John gave him ten pounds and he drank it up all in a week.

Sir John sent far and wide to find Tom's father and mother, but he might have looked till Doomsday for them, for one was dead and the other was in Australia's Botany Bay. And the little girl would not play with her dolls for a whole week, and never forgot poor little Tom. And soon my lady put a pretty tombstone over Tom's shell in the little churchyard in Vendale, where the old people of the dales all sleep side by side between the limestone crags. And the dame decked it with garlands every Sunday till she grew so old that she could not go out at all, and then the little children decked it for her. And always she sang an old, old song as she sat spinning what she called her wedding dress. The children could not understand it, but they liked it in spite of that, for it was very sweet and very sad, and that was enough for them. And these are the words:

"When all the world is young, lad,
  And all the trees are green;
And every goose a swan, lad,
  And every lass a queen;
Then hey for boot and horse, lad,
  And round the world away;
Young blood must have its course, lad,
  And every dog his day.

"When all the world is old, lad,
  And all the trees are brown;
And all the sport is stale, lad,
  And all the wheels run down;
Creep home, and take your place there,
  The spent and maimed among:
God grant you find one face there,
  You loved when all was young."

Those are the words, but they are only the body of it. The soul of the song was the dear old woman's sweet face, and sweet voice, and the sweet old air to which she sang; and that, alas! one cannot put on paper. And at last she grew so stiff and lame that the angles were forced to carry her away; and they helped her on with her wedding dress and carried her up over Harthover Fells, and a long way beyong that too; and there was a new schoolmistress in Vendale, and we will hope that the children loved her.

And all the while Tom was swimming in the river with a pretty little lace collar of gills around his neck, as lively as a grig and as clean as a fresh salmon.

Now, if you don't like my story, then go to the schoolroom and learn your multiplication table and see if you like that better. Some people would. So much the better for us, if not for them. It takes all sorts, they say, to make a world.

When they arrived at the school, all the children came out to look (page 64)

In fact, the fairies had turned him into a water-baby
(page 66)

CHAPTER THREE

RIVER LIFE

Tom was now fully amphibious. You do not know what that means?

You had better, then, ask the nearest university student, who may possibly answer you smartly in this way:

"Amphibious. Adjective, derived from two Greek words, *amphi,* a fish, and *bios,* a beast. An animal supposed by our unscientific ancestors to be compounded of a fish and a beast; which therefore, like the hippopotamus, can't live on the land and dies in the water."

However that may be, Tom was amphibious and, what is better still, he was clean.

He did not remember having ever been dirty. Indeed, he did not remember any of his old troubles, being tired, or hungry, or beaten, or sent up dark chimneys. Since that sweep sleep, he had forgotten all about his master, and Harthover Place, and the pretty little girl, and, in fact, everything that had happened to him when he lived before; and what was best of all, he had forgotten all the bad words which he had learned from Grimes and the rude boys with whom he used to play.

That is not strange for, you know, when you came into this world and became a land-baby, you remembered nothing. So why should he, when he became a water-baby?

Then have you lived before?

My dear child, who can tell? One can only tell that by remembering something which happened where we lived before; and as we remember nothing, we know nothing about it, and no book, and no person can ever tell us certainly.

There was a wise man once, a very wise man, and a very good man, who wrote a poem about the feelings which some children have about having lived before and this is what he said:

"Our birth is but a sleep and a forgetting;
The soul that rises with us, our life's star,
Hath elsewhere had its setting,
And cometh from afar:
Not in entire forgetfulness,
And not in utter nakedness,
But trailing clouds of glory, do we come
From God, who is our home."

There, you can know no more than that. But if I was you, I would believe that.

For then the great fairy Science, who is likely to be queen of all the fairies for many a year to come, can only do you good, and never do you harm; and instead of imagining, with some people, that your body makes your soul, as if a steam engine could make its own coke; or, with some people, that your soul has nothing to do with your body, but is only stuck into it like a pin into a pincushion, to fall out with the first shake, you will believe the one true,

orthodox,
rational,
philosophical,
inductive,
deductive,
seductive,
logical,
irrefragable,
nominalistic,
realistic,
productive,
salutary,
comfortable,
and on-all-accounts-to-be received

doctrine of this wonderful fairy tale: which is that

your soul actually makes your body, just as the snail makes its own shell.

For the rest, it is enough for us to believe that whether or not we lived before, we shall certainly live again, though not, I hope, as poor little orphaned Tom did. For he went downward into the water where he became clean again, and eventually lived his life in a better way; but we, I hope, shall go directly upward to a very different kind of place.

And Tom was very happy in the water.

He had been sadly overworked in the land-world; and so, now, to make up for that, he had nothing but holidays in the water-world for a long time to come.

He had nothing to do now but enjoy himself, and look at all the pretty things which are to be seen in the cool, clear water-world, where the sun is never too hot and the frost is never too cold, and everything is just as it should be.

And what did he live on? Water-cress, perhaps? Or maybe he had water-gruel mixed with water-milk? But that does not sound very tasty, so I rather expect there was some more delicious food than that in the water-world. But we do not know what one-tenth of the water-things eat, so we cannot really say – or even try to guess what kind of food the water-babies lived on.

And how did Tom pass the time in his new water-world? Sometimes he went along the smooth gravel waterways looking at the crickets which ran in and out among the stones as rabbits do on land.

Sometimes he climbed over the ledges of rock, and saw the formations that looked to him like the long, thin pipes of an organ.

On some days he went into a quiet corner and watched the caddis flies eating dead sticks as greedily as you would eat plum pudding. He watched them, too, building their houses of silk and glue. Very imaginative builders were these female caddis flies, for they liked variety and none of them would keep to the same materials for more than one day.

One would begin with some pebbles; then she would stick on a piece of green wood; then she found a shell and stuck it on top. But the poor shell was still alive, and did not like being taken to build houses with. The caddis fly, however, did not let it have any choice in the matter, being rude and selfish, as vain people are apt to be. Then she stuck on a piece of rotten wood, then a very smart pink stone, and so on, until the house was patched all over like a poor person's coat.

The caddis fly then stopped for a while to admire her work as a builder.

Then she found a long straw, five times as long as herself, and said, "Hurrah! my sister has a tail, and I'll have one too." And she stuck it on her back and marched around with it most proudly, though it was very inconvenient indeed.

After that, such tails became all the fashion among the caddis flies in that pool, just as they did in our Long Pond last May, and they all toddled around with long straws sticking out behind, getting between each other's legs, and tumbling over each other, and looking so ridiculous that Tom laughed at them till he cried, as we did. But they were quite right, you know, for people must always follow the fashion, even if it is silly and vain and makes people laugh at them until they cry.

Then sometimes he came to a deep, still reach and there he saw the water-forests. You would have seen them only as little weeds; but Tom, you must remember, was so little that everything looked a hundred times as big to him as it does to you, just as things do to a minnow, who sees and catches the little water-creatures which you can only see in a microscope. And the water-forests swayed back and forth with the movement of the water.

And in the water-forest he saw the water-monkeys and water-squirrels (they all had six legs, though;

almost everything has six legs in the water except efts and water-babies); and nimbly they ran among the branches. There were water-flowers there too, in thousands, and Tom tried to pick them; but as soon as he touched them, they drew themselves in and turned into knots of jelly; and then Tom saw that they were all alive: bells, and stars, and wheels, and flowers, of all beautiful shapes and shades, and all alive and busy, just as Tom was. So now he found that there was a great deal more in the world than he had thought at first sight.

There was one wonderful little fellow who peeped out of the top of a house built of round bricks. He had two big wheels and one little one, with teeth all over, spinning round and round like the wheels in a threshing machine; and Tom stood and stared at him to see what he was going to make with his machinery. And what do you think he was doing? Brick making! With his two big wheels he swept together all the mud which floated in the water. All that was nice in it he put into his stomach and ate, and all the mud he put into the little wheel on his breast, which really was a round hole set with teeth; and there he spun it into a neat, hard round brick. Then he took it and stuck it on the top of the wall of his house, and set to work to make another. Now was he not a clever fellow?

Tom thought so; but when he wanted to talk to him, the brick maker was much too busy and proud of his work to take notice.

Now, you must know that all the things under the water talk, not in a language like ours, but like horses, and dogs, and cows, and birds talk to each other; and Tom soon learned to understand them and talk to them. So he might have had very pleasant company if he had only been a good boy. But I am sorry to say, he was too like some other little boys, very fond of hunting and tormenting creatures for mere sport. Some people say that boys cannot help it, that it is nature, and only proof that we are all originally descended from beasts of prey. But whether it is nature or not, little boys can help it, and must help it. For if they have naughty, mischievous tricks in their nature, as monkeys have, that is no reason why they should give way to those tricks like monkeys, who know no better. And therefore they must not torment dumb creatures, for, if they do, a certain old lady who is coming will surely give them exactly what they deserve.

But Tom did not know that, and he nipped and pushed the poor water-things all the time, till they were afraid and got out of his way or crept into their shells. So he had no one to speak to or play with.

The water-fairies, of course, were very sorry to see him so unhappy, and longed to take him aside and tell him how naughty he was, and teach him to be good, and then to play and romp with him, but they had been forbidden to do that. Tom had to learn his lesson for himself through his own experience, as many another foolish person has to do, though there may be many a kind heart yearning over them all the while, and longing to teach them what they can only teach themselves.

At last, one day he found a caddis fly and wanted it to peep out of its house, but its door was shut. He had never seen a caddis house with a door before, so what must he do, the meddlesome little fellow, but pull it open to see what the poor lady was doing inside.

What a shame! How would you like to have someone breaking your bedroom door in to see how you looked when you were in bed? So Tom broke down the door, which was the prettiest little grating of silk stuck all over the shining bits of crystal; and when he looked in, the caddis poked out her head, which had turned into just the shape of a bird's. But when Tom spoke to her she could not answer, for her mouth and face were tied up tight in a new nightcap of neat pink skin. However, though she couldn't answer, all the other caddises did. They held up their hands and shrieked like the cats in Struwelpeter:

Oh, you nasty, horrid boy; there you are at it again! And she had just snuggled down for a couple of week's sleep, and then she would have come out with such beautiful wings, and flown everywhere, and laid lots of eggs; and now you have broken her door, and she can't mend it because her mouth is tied up for her sleep, and she will die. Who sent you here to worry us out of our lives?"

So Tom swam away. He was very much ashamed of himself and felt all the naughtier, as little boys do when they have done wrong and won't say so.

Then he came to a pool full of little trout and began tormenting them and trying to catch them; but they slipped through his fingers and jumped all the way out of the water in their fright. But as Tom chased them, he came close to a great, dark hole under an alder root, and out flashed a huge old brown trout, ten times as big as he was, and ran right against him and knocked all the breath out of his body; and I don't know which was the more frightened of the two.

Then Tom went on sulky and lonely, as he deserved to be; and under a bank he saw a very strange dirty creature sitting, about half as big as himself. It had six legs, and a big stomach, and a most ridiculous head with two great eyes, and a face just like a donkey's.

"Oh!" said Tom, "you are an ugly fellow, to be sure!" and he began making faces at it and put his nose close to it, and yelled at it, like a very rude boy.

When, hey presto! the thing's donkey face came off in a moment, and out popped a long arm with a pair of pincers at the end of it, and caught Tom by the nose. It did not hurt him much, but it held him tightly.

"Yah, ah! Oh, let me go!" cried Tom.

"Then let me alone," said the creature. "I want to be quiet. I want to split."

Tom promised to let him alone, and it let go of his nose.

"Why do you want to split?" said Tom.

"Because my brothers and sisters have all split, and turned into beautiful creatures with wings, so I want to split too. Don't speak to me. I am sure I shall split. I will split!"

Tom stood still and watched. And it swelled itself, and puffed, and stretched itself out stiff, and at last – crack, puff, bang! it opened all down its back, and then up to the top of its head.

And out of its inside came a most slender, elegant, soft creature, as soft and smooth as Tom, but very pale and weak, like a little child who has been ill a long time in a dark room. It moved its legs very feebly, and looked all around half ashamed, like a girl when she goes into a ballroom for the first time; and then it began walking slowly up a grass stem to the top of the water.

Tom was so astonished that he never said a word, but he stared with all his eyes. And he went up to the top of the water too, and peeped out to see what would happen.

As the creature sat in the warm, bright sun, a wonderul change came over it. It grew strong and firm, the most lovely hues began to show on its body, blue and yellow and black, spots and bars and rings; out of its back rose four great wings of bright brown gauze, and its eyes grew so large that they filled all its head, and shone like ten thousand diamonds.

"Oh, you beautiful creature!" said Tom and he put out his hand to catch it.

But the thing whirred up into the air, hung poised on its wings a moment, and then fearlessly settled down again by Tom.

"No!" it said, "you cannot catch me. I am a dragonfly now, the king of all the flies; and I shall dance in the sunshine and hawk over the river, and catch gnats, and have a beautiful wife like myself. I know what I shall do. Hurrah!" And he flew away into the air and began catching gnats.

"Oh! come back, come back," cried Tom, "you beautiful creature. I have no one to play with, and I am so lonely here. If you will only come back, I promise I will never try to catch you."

"I don't care whether you do or not," said the dragonfly, "for you can't. But when I have had my dinner and looked around this pretty place a little, I will come back and have a little chat about all I have seen in my travels."

The dragonfly did come back and chatted away with Tom. He was a little conceited about his fine tints and his large wings, but, you know, he had been a poor, dirty, ugly creature all his life before, so there was some excuse for him. He was very fond of talking about all the wonderful things he saw in the trees and the meadows, and Tom liked to listen, for he had forgotten all about them. So, in a little while, they became great friends.

I am very glad to say that Tom learned a good lesson that day and did not torment creatures for a long time after. Then the caddis flies grew quite tame, and used to tell him strange stories about the way they built their houses, and changed their skins, and turned at last into winged flies. This made Tom wish that he could change his skin, and have wings like them some day.

Then the trout and he made up, for trout very soon forget if they have been frightened and hurt. So Tom used to play with the trout at hare and hounds, and great fun they had. He used to try to leap out of the water, head over heels, as they did before a shower came on, but somehow he never could manage it.

He liked most, though, to see the fish rising at the flies, as they sailed round and round under the shadow of the great oak, where the beetles fell flop into the water, and the green caterpillars let themselves down from the boughs by silk ropes for no reason at all, and then changed their foolish minds for no reason at all, either, and hauled themselves up again into the tree, rolling up the rope in a ball between their paws. This is a very clever rope dancer's trick, and not even Blondin or Leotard, the famous performers, could do it; but why the caterpillars should take so much trouble about it no one can tell, for they cannot earn their living, as Blondin and Leotard did, by trying to break their necks on a string.

Very often Tom caught them just as they touched the water, and also caught the alder flies and the caddises, and the cocktailed duns and spinners of yellow, and brown, and claret, and gave them to his friends, the trout. Perhaps this was not kind to the flies, but one must do a good turn to one's friends when one can.

At last he even gave up catching the flies, for he made the acquaintanceship of one by accident, and found him a very merry little fellow. Now, this was the way it happened, and it is all really true.

He was basking at the top of the water one hot day in July, catching duns and feeding the trout, when he saw a new sort, a dark little fellow with a brown head. He was a very little fellow, indeed, but he made the most of himself, as people ought to do. He cocked up his head, and he cocked up his wings, and he cocked up his tail, and he cocked up the two whisks at the end of his tail, and, in short, he looked the cockiest of all the cocky. And so he proved to be, for, instead of flying away, he hopped upon Tom's finger and sat there as bold as nine tailors; and he cried out in the tiniest, shrillest, squeakiest little voice you ever heard:

"Much obliged to you, indeed; but I don't want it yet."

"Want what?" said Tom, who was taken aback by such impudence.

"Your leg, which you are kind enough to hold out

for me to sit on. I must just go and see after my wife for a few minutes. Dear me! what a troublesome business a family is!" (though the idle little rogue did nothing at all, but left his poor wife to lay all the eggs by herself). "When I come back, I shall be glad if you'll be so good as to keep it sticking out just as it is now." And off he flew.

Tom thought him a very cool sort of creature, and still more so when, in five minutes, he came back and said, "Ah, you were tired waiting? Well, your other leg will do as well."

He popped himself down on Tom's knee and began chatting away in his squeaking voice.

"So you live under the water? It's a low, deep place. I lived there for some time and was very shabby and dirty. But I decided to change my style. So I turned respectable, and came up to the top, and put on this dark suit. It's a very businesslike suit, don't you think?"

"Very neat and quiet indeed," said Tom.

"Yes. One must be quiet, and neat, and respectable, and all that sort of thing when one becomes a family man. But I'm tired of it, that's the truth. I've done quite enough business, I consider, in the last week, to last me my life. So I shall put on a smart suit and go out and be a man about town, and see the

There are land-babies. Then why not water-babies?
(page 67)

The fairies washed him in the river, and the pretty little real Tom swam away (page 69)

wide world, and have a dance or two. Why shouldn't one be jolly if one can?"

And as he spoke he turned very pale and then completely white.

"Why, you're ill!" said Tom. But the fly did not answer.

"You're dead," said Tom, looking at him as he stood on his knee as white as a ghost.

"No I ain't!" answered a little squeaking voice over his head. "This is me up here, in my dance suit, and that's my skin. Ha, ha! you could not do such a trick as that!"

And, indeed, Tom could not, nor could Houdini, nor Robin, nor Frikell, nor all the magicians in the world. For the little rogue had jumped right out of his own skin and left it standing on Tom's knee: eyes, wings, legs, tail, exactly as if it had been alive.

"Ha, ha!" he said, and he jumped, and he jerked, and skipped up and down, never stopping an instant, just as if he couldn't stop. "Ain't I a pretty fellow now?"

And so he was, for his body was white, and his tail orange, and his eyes all the shades of a peacock's tail. And the oddest thing of all was that the whisks at the end of his tail had grown five times as long as they were before.

"Ah!" said he, "now I will see the wide world. My living expenses won't be much, for I have no mouth, you see, and no inside, so I can never be hungry or have a stomach ache, either."

And this was so. He had grown as dry and hard and empty as a quill, as such silly, shallow-hearted fellows deserve to be.

But, instead of being ashamed of his emptiness, he was proud of it, as a good many fine gentlemen and ladies are, and began jerking and flipping up and down, and singing:

"My wife shall dance and I shall sing,
So merrily pass the day;
For I hold it for quite the wisest thing,
To drive dull care away."

And he danced up and down for three days and three nights, till he grew so tired that he tumbled into the water and went under. But what became of him, Tom never knew, and he himself never minded, for Tom heard him singing to the last as he vanished:

"To drive dull care away-ay-ay!"

But one day Tom had a new adventure. He was

sitting on a waterlily leaf, he and his friend the dragonfly, watching the gnats dance. The dragonfly had eaten as many as he wanted, and was sitting still and sleepy, for it was very hot and bright. The gnats, who did not care the least for their poor brothers' death, danced happily, about a foot over his head, and a large black fly settled within an inch of his nose and began washing his own face and combing his hair with his paws; but the dragonfly never stirred, and kept on chatting to Tom about the times when he lived under the water.

Suddenly, Tom heard the strangest noise upstream, cooing, and grunting, and whining, and squeaking, as if you had put two stock doves, nine mice, three guineapigs, and a blind puppy into a bag, and left them there to settle themselves and make music.

He looked up that way and there he saw a sight as strange as the noise: a great ball rolling over and over down the stream, seeming one moment to be soft brown fur, and the next shining glass; and yet it was not a ball, for sometimes it broke up and streamed away in pieces, and then it joined again; and all the while the noise came out of it louder and louder.

Tom asked the dragonfly what it could be, but, of course, with his bad sight he could not even see it, though it was not ten yards away. So Tom took the neatest little dive into the water and started off to see for himself; and when he came near, the ball turned out to be four or five beautiful creatures, many times larger than Tom, who were swimming and rolling, and diving and twisting, and wrestling and cuddling, and kissing and biting, and scratching, in the most charming fashion that ever was seen.

But when the biggest of them saw Tom, she darted out from the rest, and cried in water-language most sharply, "Quick, children, here is something good to eat," and came at poor Tom, showing such a wicked pair of eyes and such a sharp set of teeth in a grinning mouth, that Tom, who had thought her very handsome, said to himself, "Handsome is as handsome does," and slipped in between the waterlily roots as fast as he could. Then he turned around and made faces at her.

"Come out," said the mother otter, "or it will be worse for you."

But Tom looked at her from between two thick roots and shook them with all his might, making horrible faces all the while, just as he used to grin through fence railings at old women on land. It was not behaving in a well-bred way, no doubt; but, you know, Tom had not finished his education yet.

"Come away, children," said the otter in disgust. "It is not worth eating after all. It is only a nasty eft, which no creature eats, not even those vulgar pikes in the pond."

"I am not an eft!" said Tom. "Efts have tails."

"You are an eft," said the otter, very positively. "I see your two hands quite plain, and I know you have a tail."

"I tell you I have not," said Tom. "Look here," and he turned his pretty little self completely around, and, sure enough, he no more had a tail on his body than you do.

The otter might have made the best of it by saying that Tom was a frog; but, like a great many other people, when she had once said a thing, she stuck to it right or wrong. So she answered: "I say you are an eft, and therefore you are, and not fit food for gentlefolk like me and my children. You may stay there till the salmon eat you." She knew the salmon would not, but she wanted to frighten poor Tom. "Ha! ha! they will eat you, and we will eat them." And the otter laughed such a wicked, cruel laugh, as you may hear them do sometimes, and the first time that you hear it you will probably think it is bogeys.

"What are salmon?" asked Tom.

"Fish, you eft, great fish, nice fish to eat. They are

the lords of the fish, and we are lords of the salmon;" and she laughed again. "We hunt them up and down the pools and drive them into a corner, the silly things. They are so proud, and bully the little trout and the minnows till they see us coming, and then they are so meek all at once; and we catch them, but we disdain to eat them all. We just bite out their soft throats and suck their sweet juice, oh, so good!" And she licked her wicked lips, "and then throw them away, and go and catch another. They are coming soon, children, coming soon. I can smell the rain coming off the sea, and then hurrah for fresh salmon, and plenty of eating all day long."

"And where do they come from?" asked Tom, who kept himself safe in the roots, for he was truly frightened.

"Out of the sea, eft, the great, wide sea, where they could stay and be safe if they had sense. But out of the sea the silly things come, into the great river down below, and we come up to watch for them; and when they go down again, we go down and follow them. And there we fish for the bass and the pollock, and have jolly days along the shore, and toss and roll in the breakers, and sleep snug in the warm dry crags. Ah, life would indeed be merry, children, if it were not for those horrid men."

"What are men?" asked Tom; but somehow he seemed to know before he asked.

"Two-legged things, eft; and, now I come to look at you, they are actually something like you, if you did not have a tail" (she was determined to believe that Tom had a tail), "only a great deal bigger, worse luck for us; and they catch the fish with hooks and lines, which get into our feet sometimes, and set pots along the rocks to catch lobsters. They speared my poor dear husband as he went out to find something for us to eat. I was laid up among the crags then, and we were very low in the world, for the sea was so rough that no fish would come inshore. But they speared him, poor fellow, and I saw them carrying him away upon a pole. Ah, he lost his life for your sakes, my children, poor, dear, obedient creature that he was."

And the otter grew so sentimental (for otters can be very sentimental when they choose, like a good many people who are both cruel and greedy, and no good to anybody at all) that she sailed solemnly away down the burn, and Tom saw her no more for that time. And lucky it was for her that she did so, for no sooner was she gone than down the bank came seven little rough terrier dogs, snuffing, and yapping, and grubbing, and splashing in full cry after the otter.

Tom hid among the waterlilies till they were gone, for he could not guess that they were the water-fairies come to help him.

But he could not help thinking of what the otter had said about the great river and the broad sea. And as he thought, he longed to go and see them. He could not tell why, but the more he thought about it, the more discontented he grew with the narrow little stream in which he lived, and all his companions there. He wanted to get out into the wide, wide world and enjoy all the wonderful sights he was sure filled it.

Once he actually started to go down the stream. But the stream was very low, and when he came to the shallows, he could not keep under water, for there was no water left to keep under. So the sun burned his back and made him sick; and he went back again and lay quiet in the pool for a whole week long.

And then, on the evening of a very hot day, he saw an amazing sight.

He had been very sluggish all day, and so had the trout, for they would not move an inch to take a fly though there were thousands on the water, but lay dozing at the bottom under the shade of the stones. Tom lay dozing too, and was glad to cuddle their cool sides, for the water was too warm to be pleasant.

Toward evening it suddenly grew dark, and Tom looked up and saw a blanket of black clouds lying right across the valley above his head, resting on the crags right and left. He felt not exactly frightened, but went very still, for everything was still. There was not a whisper of wind, nor a chirp of a bird to be heard; and next a few great drops of rain fell plop into the water, and one hit Tom on the nose and made him pop his head down quickly.

And then the thunder roared, and the lightning flashed, leaping across Vendale and back again from cloud to cloud and cliff to cliff, till the very rocks in the stream seemed to shake; and Tom looked up at it through the water, and thought it the finest thing he had ever seen in his life.

But he dared not put his head out of the water, for the rain came down by bucketfuls, and the hail hammered like gunshot on the stream and churned it into foam; and soon the stream rose and rushed along, higher and higher, and fouler and fouler, full of beetles, and sticks, and straws, and worms, and addle eggs, and woodlice, and leeches, and odds and ends, and omnium gatherums, and this, that, and the other, enough to fill nine museums.

Tom could hardly stand against the flow of the stream and hid behind a rock. But the trout did not, for out they rushed from among the stones and began gobbling the beetles and leeches in the most greedy and quarrelsome way, and then swam around with great worms hanging out of the sides of their mouths, tugging and kicking to get them away from each other.

And now, by the flashes of lightning, Tom saw a new sight: all the bottom of the stream was alive with great eels, turning and twisting along, all down stream and away. They had been hiding for weeks past in the cracks of the rocks and in burrows in the mud, and Tom had hardly ever seen them except now and then at night; but now they were all out, and went hurrying past him so fiercely and wildly that he was frightened. And as they hurried past he could hear them say to each other, "We must run, we must run. What a jolly thunderstorm! Down to the sea, down to the sea!"

And then the otter came by with all her brood, twining and sweeping along as fast as the eels themselves. She spied Tom as she came by and said to him:

"Now is your time, eft, if you want to see the world. Come along, children, never mind those nasty eels. We shall breakfast on salmon tomorrow. Down to the sea, down to the sea!"

Then came a flash brighter than all the rest, and by the light of it, Tom was certain he saw three beautiful little girls, though they were gone again in the thousandth part of a second. Yet he was sure he had seen them; they had their arms twined around each other's necks and were floating down the torrent as they sang, "Down to the sea, down to the sea!"

"Oh, stay! Wait for me!" cried Tom; but they were gone. Yet he could hear their voices clear and sweet through the roar of thunder and water and wind, singing "Down to the sea!" till they died away.

"Down to the sea?" said Tom. "Everything is going to the sea, and I will too. Goodbye, trout." But the trout never turned to answer, so Tom was spared the pain of bidding farewell to them.

And now, down the rushing stream, guided by the bright flashes of the storm; past tall birch-fringed rocks which shone out one moment as clear as day and were dark as night the next, past dark holes under swirling banks from which huge trout rushed out on Tom, thinking him to be good to eat, and turned back sulkily, for the fairies sent them home again with a tremendous scolding, for daring to meddle with a water-baby (Tom did not know that the fairies were always close to him); on through narrow straights and roaring cataracts, where Tom was deafened and blinded for a moment by the rushing waters; along deep reaches, where the white waterlilies tossed and flapped beneath the wind and hail; past sleeping villages; under dark bridge arches, and away and away to the sea. And Tom could not stop, and did not want to stop. He would see the great world below, and the salmon, and the breakers, and the wide, wide sea.

And when the daylight came, Tom found himself out in the salmon river.

But Tom was not the least interested in the river. All he wanted was to get down to the wide, wide sea.

After a while he came to a place where the river spread out into broad, still, shallow reaches, so wide that little Tom, as he put his head out of the water, could hardly see across.

And there he stopped, for he had become a little frightened. "This must be the sea," he thought. "What a wide place it is! If I go into it, I shall surely lose my way, or some strange thing will bite me. I will stop here and look out for the otter, or the eels, or someone to tell me where I should go."

So he went back a little way and crept into a crack of the rock, just where the river opened out into the wide shallows, and watched for someone to show him the way; but the otter and the eels were miles and miles down the stream ahead of him.

There he waited, and slept too, for he was tired after his night's journey; and when he woke, the stream was clearing to a beautiful amber hue, though it was still very high. And after a while he saw a sight which made him jump up, for he knew in a moment it was one of the things which he had come to look for.

Such a fish! Ten times as big as the biggest trout, and a hundred times as big as Tom was, sculling up the stream past him, as easily as Tom had sculled down.

Such a fish! Shining silver from head to tail, and here and there a crimson dot, with a grand hooked nose and a grand curling lip, and a grand bright eye, looking round him as proudly as a king, and surveying the water right and left as if all belonged to him. Surely he must be the salmon, the king of all the fish.

Tom was so frightened that he longed to creep into a hole, but he need not have been so scared. For salmon are all true gentlefolk, and, like true gentlefolk they look noble and proud, yet, like true gentlefolk, they never harm or quarrel with anyone, but go about their own business and leave other people to themselves.

The salmon looked at him full in the face and then went on without paying him attention, with a swish or two of his tail which made the stream boil again. And in a few minutes came another, and then four or five, and so on, and all passed Tom, rushing and plunging up the cataract with strong strokes of their silver tails, now and then leaping right out of the water and up over a rock, shining gloriously for a moment in the bright sun. Tom was so delighted that he could have watched them all day long.

And at last came one bigger than all the rest, but he came slowly and stopped, and looked back, and seemed very anxious and busy. Then Tom saw that he was helping another salmon, an especially handsome one, who had not a single spot upon it, but was clothed in pure silver from nose to tail.

"My dear," said the large fish to his companion, "you really look dreadfully tired, and you must not over exert yourself at first. Do rest yourself behind this rock." And he shoved her gently with his nose, to the rock where Tom sat.

You must know that this was the salmon's wife. For salmon, like other true gentlemen, always choose their lady, and love her, and are true to her, and take care of her, and work for her, and fight for her, as every true gentleman ought. They are not like vulgar chub, and roach, and pike, who have no gentle feelings and do not take care of their wives.

Then he saw Tom and looked at him very fiercely for a moment, as if he was going to bite.

"What do you want here?" he said, very fiercely.

"Oh, don't hurt me!" cried Tom. "I only want to look at you. You are so handsome."

"Ah!" said the salmon, very stately, but very civilly. "I really beg your pardon; I see what you are, my little dear. I have met one or two creatures like you before, and found them very agreeable and well-behaved. Indeed, one of them showed me a great kindness lately, which I hope to be able to repay. I hope we shall not be in your way here. As soon as my wife is rested, we shall proceed on our journey."

"So you have seen things like me before?" asked Tom.

"Several times, my dear. Indeed, it was only last night that one at the river's mouth came and warned me and my wife of some new stake nets which had got into the stream, I cannot tell how, since last winter, and showed us the way round them, in the most charmingly obliging way."

"So there are babies in the sea?" cried Tom, and clapped his hands. "Then I shall have someone to play with. How delightful!"

"Were there no babies where you were?" asked the lady salmon.

"No! and I grew so lonely. I thought I saw three last night, but they were gone in an instant, down to the sea. So I went too, for I had nothing to play with but dragonflies and trout."

"Ugh!" she cried "what low company!"

"My dear, if he has been in low company, he has certainly not learned their low manners," said the salmon.

"No, indeed, poor little dear; but how sad for him to live among such as caddises, the nasty things; and dragonflies, too! Why, they are not even good to eat, for they are all hard and empty; and, as for trout, everyone knows what they are." Whereon she curled up her lip, and looked dreadfully scornful, while her husband curled up his too.

"Why do you dislike the trout so?" asked Tom.

"My dear, we do not even mention them if we can help it, for I am sorry to say they are relatives of ours who do us no credit. A great many years ago they were just like us, but they were so lazy, and cowardly, and greedy, that instead of going down to the sea every year to see the world and grow strong and fat, they choose to stay and poke around in the little streams and eat worms and grubs; and they are

Tom was so little that everything looked a hundred times as big to him (page 80)

"I am a dragonfly now, the king of all the flies" (page 86)

very properly punished for it, for they have grown ugly, and brown, and spotted, and small, and are actually so degraded in their tastes that they will eat our children."

"And then they pretend to scrape acquaintance with us again," said the lady. "Why, I have actually known one of them to propose to a lady salmon, the impudent little creature."

"I should hope," said the gentleman, "that there are very few female salmon who would bother listening to such a creature for an instant. If I saw such a thing happen, I would consider it my duty to put them both to death on the spot." So the old salmon said, like an old blue-blooded hidalgo of Spain; and what is more, he would have done it too. For, you must know, no enemies are so bitter against each other as those who are of the same blood and race; and a salmon looks on a trout, as some great folk look on some little folk, as something just too much like himself to be tolerated.

Hilda.T. Miller

CHAPTER FOUR

DOWN TO THE SEA

So the salmon went up, after Tom had warned them of the wicked old otter; and Tom went down, but slowly and cautiously, coasting along the shore. He was many days about it, for it was many miles down to the sea, and perhaps he would never have found his way if the fairies had not guided him, without his seeing their fair faces, or feeling their gentle hands.

And, as he went, he had a strange adventure. It was a clear, still September night, and the moon shone down so brightly through the water that he could not sleep, though he shut his eyes as tight as possible. So at last he came up to the top and sat upon a little point of rock, and looked up at the broad yellow moon, and wondered what she was, and thought that she looked at him. And he watched the moonlight on the rippling river, and the black heads of the firs, and the silver-frosted lawns, and listened to the owl's hoot, and the snipe's bleat, and the fox's bark, and the otter's laugh; and smelled the soft perfume of the birches, and the wafts of heather honey off the grouse moor far above; and felt very happy, though he could not well tell why. You, of course, would have been very cold sitting there on your wet back, but Tom was a water-baby and therefore did not feel the cold.

Suddenly, he saw a beautiful sight. A bright red light moved along the riverside and threw down into the water a long tap-root of flame. Tom, curious little rogue that he was, just had to go and see what it was, so he swam to the shore and met the light as it stopped over a shallow run at the edge of a low rock.

And there, underneath the light, lay five or six huge salmon, looking up at the flame with their great goggle eyes and wagging their tails as if they were very much pleased with it.

Tom came to the top to look at this wonderful light nearer, and made a splash.

And he heard a voice say:

"A fish just rose."

He did not know what the words meant, but he seemed to know the sound of them and to know the voice which spoke them; and he saw on the bank three big two-legged creatures, one of whom held the light, flaring and sputtering, and another a long pole. And he knew that they were men, and was frightened, and crept into a hole in the rock from which he could see what went on.

The man with the torch bent down over the water, and looked earnestly in; and then he said:

"Tak' that muckle fellow, lad; he's ower fifteen punds; and haud your hand steady."

Tom felt that there was some danger coming and longed to warn the foolish salmon, who kept staring up at the bright light as if bewitched. But before he could make up his mind, down came the pole through the water. There was a fearful splash and struggle, and Tom saw that the poor salmon was speared right through, and was lifted out of the water.

And then, from behind, there sprang on these three men three other men; and there were shouts, and blows, and words which Tom thought he had heard before; and he shuddered and turned sick at them now, for he felt somehow that they were strange, and ugly, and wrong, and horrible. And it all began to come back to him. They were men and they were fighting; savage, desperate, up-and-down fighting, such as Tom had seen too many times before.

And he covered his little ears and longed to swim away, and was very glad that he was a water-baby and had nothing to do any more with horrid dirty men, with foul clothes on their backs, and foul words on their lips; but he dared not stir out of his hole while the rock shook over his head with the trampling and struggling of the keepers and the poachers.

All of a sudden, there was a tremendous splash, and a frightful flash, and a hissing, and then all was still.

For, into the water close to Tom fell one of the men, the one who held the light in his hand. Into the swift river he sank, and rolled over and over in the current. Tom heard the men above run along, seemingly looking for him; but he drifted down into the deep hole below, and there lay without moving, and they could not find him.

Tom waited a long time, till all was quiet and then he peeped out and saw the man where he lay. He screwed up his courage and swam to him. "Perhaps," he thought, "the water has made him fall asleep, as it did me."

Then he went nearer. He grew more and more curious, he could not tell why. He had to go and look at him. He would go very quietly, of course; so he swam round and round him, closer and closer; and, as he did not stir, at last Tom came very close and looked him in the face.

The moon shone so bright that Tom could see every feature; and, as he looked, he remembered the man as his old master, Grimes.

Tom turned tail and swam away as fast as he could.

"Oh, dear me!" he thought, "now he will turn into a water-baby. What a nasty, troublesome one he will be! And perhaps he will meet up with me and beat me again."

So he went up the river again a little way, and lay there the rest of the night under an alder root; but, when morning came, he longed to go down again to the big pool and see whether Mr. Grimes had turned into a water-baby yet.

So he went very carefully, peeping round all the rocks and hiding under all the roots. Mr. Grimes lay there still; he had not turned into a water-baby. In the afternoon Tom went back again. He could not rest till he had found out what had become of Mr. Grimes. But this time Mr. Grimes was gone, and Tom made up his mind that he was turned into a water-baby.

He did not need to worry, poor little man. Mr.

Grimes did not turn into a water-baby, or anything like one at all. But Tom could not feel easy, and for a long time he was fearful that he would meet Grimes suddenly in some deep pool. He could not know that the fairies had carried him away, and put him, where they put everything which falls into the water, exactly where it ought to be.

Then Tom went on down stream, for he was afraid of staying near Grimes, following the flow of the stream day after day, past large bridges, past boats and barges, past the great town with its wharfs, and mills, and tall smoking chimneys, and ships which rode at anchor in the stream. Now and then he ran against their hawsers, and wondered what they were, and peeped out, and saw the sailors lounging on board smoking their pipes, and ducked under again, for he was terribly afraid of being caught by man and turned into a chimney sweep once more.

He did not know that the fairies were guarding him always, shutting the sailors' eyes so they wouldn't see him, and turning him aside from mill races, and sewer mouths, and all foul and dangerous things. Poor little fellow, it was a dreary journey for him, and more than once he longed to be back in Vendale, playing with the trout in the bright summer sun.

But Tom was always a brave, determined, little English bulldog, who never knew when he was beaten; and on and on he went, till he saw the red buoy a long way off through the fog. And then to his surprise, he found the stream had turned round and ran up inland.

It was the tide, of course, but Tom knew nothing of the tide. He only knew that in a minute more the water, which had been fresh, turned salt all round him. And then there came a change over him.

Suddenly, he felt as strong, and light, and fresh, as if he had champagne in his veins, and he gave, he did not know why, three skips out of the water a yard high, and head over heels, just as the salmon do when they first touch the noble rich salt water, which, as some wise folk tell us, is the mother of all living things.

He did not care now that the tide was against him. The red buoy was in sight, dancing in the open sea, and to the buoy he would go; and to it he went. He passed great shoals of bass and mullet, leaping and rushing in after the shrimps, but he never heeded them, or they him; and once he passed a huge black shining seal, who was coming in after the mullet. The seal put his head and shoulders out of water, and stared at him, looking very big and very fierce. And

Tom, instead of being frightened, said "How d'ye do, sir; what a beautiful place the sea is!" And the old seal, instead of trying to bite him, looked at him with his soft, sleepy, winking eyes, and said, "Good tide to you, my little man; are you looking for your brothers and sisters? I passed them all at play outside."

"Oh, then," said Tom, "I shall have playmates at last," and he swam onto the buoy, and got upon it (for he was quite out of breath) and sat there, and looked round for water-babies; but there were none to be seen.

The sea breeze came in strong with the tide and blew the fog away, and the little waves danced for joy around the buoy, and the old buoy danced with them. The shadows of the clouds ran races over the bright blue bay, and yet never caught up with each other; and the breakers plunged merrily upon the wide white sands, and jumped up over the rocks to see what the green fields inside were like, and tumbled down and broke themselves all to pieces, and never minded it a bit, but mended themselves and jumped up again. And the terns hovered over Tom like huge white dragonflies with black heads, and the gulls laughed like girls at play, and the sea pies, with their red bills and legs, flew to and fro from shore to shore and whistled sweet and wild.

Tom looked and looked and listened; and he would have been very happy, if he could only have seen the water-babies. Then when the tide turned, he left the buoy and swam round and round in search of them, but in vain. Sometimes he thought he heard them laughing, but it was only the laughter of the ripples. And sometimes he thought he saw them at the bottom: but it was only white and pink shells. And once he was sure he had found one, for he saw two bright eyes peeping out of the sand. So he dived down and began scraping the sand away, and cried,

"Don't hide. I do want someone to play with so much!" And out jumped a big turbot with his ugly eyes and mouth all awry, and flopped away along the bottom, knocking poor Tom over. And he sat down at the bottom of the sea and cried salt tears from sheer disappointment.

To have come all this way, and faced so many dangers, and yet to find no water-babies! How unfair it was!

And Tom sat on the buoy long days, long weeks, looking out to sea and wondering when the water-babies would come back; and yet they never came.

Then he began to ask all the strange things which came out of the sea if they had seen any, and some said "Yes," and some said nothing at all.

He asked the bass and the pollock, but they were in such a hurry to catch shrimps that they did not bother to answer.

Then there came a whole fleet of purple sea snails floating along, each on a sponge full of foam, and Tom said, "Where do you come from, you pretty creatures? And may I ask whether you have seen the water-babies?"

And the sea snails answered, "Whence we come we know not; and whither we are going, who can tell? We float out our life in the mid-ocean, with the warm sunshine above our heads, and the warm gulf-stream below, and that is enough for us. Yes, perhaps we have seen the water-babies. We have seen many strange things as we sailed along." And they floated away, the happy, passive things, and all went ashore upon the sands.

Then there came a large, lazy sunfish, as big as a fat pig cut in half, and he seemed to have been cut in half too, and squeezed in a clothes press till he was flat; but for all his big body and big fins he had only a little rabbit's mouth, no bigger than Tom's, and when Tom questioned him, he answered in a little, squeaky, feeble voice:

"I'm sure I don't know. I've lost my way. I meant to go to the Chesapeake, and I'm afraid I've gone wrong somehow. Dear me! it was all by following that pleasant warm water. I'm sure I've lost my way."

And when Tom asked him again, he only answered, "I've lost my way. Don't talk to me. I want to think."

But, like a good many other people, the more he tried to think, the less he could think, and Tom saw him blundering around all day, till the coastguard saw his big fin above the water, and rowed out, and struck a boathook into him, and took him away. They took him up to the town and charged a penny a head for a look at him, and made a good day's work of it. But, of course, Tom did not know that.

Then there came a shoal of porpoises, rolling as they went, papas, and mammas, and little children, and all smooth and shiny because the fairies french-polished them every morning; and they sighed so softly as they came by that Tom took courage to speak to them; but all they answered was, "Hush, hush, hush", for that was all they had ever learned to say.

And then there came a shoal of basking sharks, some of them as long as a boat, and Tom was frightened of them. But they were very lazy, good-natured creatures, not greedy tyrants like white sharks, and blue sharks, and ground sharks, and hammerheads, who eat people, or sawfish, and threshers, and ice sharks, who hunt the poor old whales. They came and rubbed their sides against the buoy, and lay basking in the sun with their back fins out of water, and winked at Tom; but he never could get them to speak. They had eaten so many herrings that they were in a trance. So Tom was glad when a collier brig came by and frightened them all away, for they certainly did smell most horribly and he had to hold his nose tight as long as they were there.

And then there came a beautiful creature, like a ribbon of pure silver, with a sharp head and very long teeth, but it seemed to be very sick and sad. Sometimes it rolled helpless on its side, and then it dashed away glittering like white fire, and then it lay motionless again, looking sick.

"Where do you come from?" asked Tom. "And why are you so sick and sad?"

"I come from the warm Carolinas and the sandbanks fringed with pines, where the great owl rays leap and flap like giant bats upon the tide. But I wandered north and north upon the treacherous, warm gulf stream, till I met with the cold icebergs afloat in the mid-ocean. So I got tangled among the icebergs and chilled with their frozen breath. But the water-babies helped me get free of them, and set me on my way again. And now I am getting better every day; but I am very sick and sad, and perhaps I shall never get home again to play with the owl rays even once more."

"Oh! cried Tom. "And you have seen water-babies? Have you seen any near here?"

"Yes, they helped me again last night, or I would have been eaten by a huge black porpoise."

How vexatious! The water-babies were close to him, and yet he could not find one.

And then he left the buoy, and used to go along the sands and round the rocks and come out in the night (like the forsaken merman in Matthew Arnold's beautiful, beautiful poem, which you must learn by heart some day) and sit upon a point of rock among the shining seaweeds in the low October tides, and cry and call for the water-babies; but he never heard a voice reply in return. And at last, his fretting and crying made him grow lean and thin.

But one day among the rocks he found a playmate. It was not a water-baby, alas! It was a lobster, and a very distinguished lobster he was, for he had live barnacles on his claws, which is a great mark of distinction in lobsterdom, and cannot be bought for money any more than a good conscience or the Victoria Cross.

Tom had never seen a lobster before and he was mightily taken with this one, for he thought it the most curious, odd, ridiculous creature he had ever seen; and there he was not far wrong, for all the ingenious people, and all the scientific people, and all the imaginative people in the world, if all their wits were boiled into one, could never invent anything so curious and so ridiculous as a lobster.

One claw was knobbed and the other was jagged, and Tom delighted in watching him hold on to the seaweed with his knobbed claw while he cut up salads with his jagged one, and then put them into his mouth after smelling at them like a monkey. And always the little barnacles threw out their casting nets and swept the water, and came in for their share of whatever there was for dinner.

But Tom was most astonished to see how he fired himself off, snap! like the leap frogs which you make out of a goose's breastbone. Certainly he took the most wonderful shots, and backwards too. For, if he wanted to go into a narrow crack ten yards off, what do you think he did? If he had gone in head foremost, of course, he could not have turned round. So he used to turn his tail to it and lay his long horns, which

Three beautiful little girls sang, "Down to the sea, down to the sea" (page 103)

Tom did not know that the fairies were always close to him
(page 103)

carry his sixth sense in their tips (and nobody knows what the sixth sense is), straight down his back to guide him, and twist his eyes back till they almost came out of their sockets, and then, like a gunshot, went fire! snap! And away he was propelled, pop into the hole, and peeped out and twiddled his whiskers, as much as to say, "You couldn't do that."

Tom asked him about water-babies. "Yes," he said. He had seen them often. But he did not think much of them. They were meddlesome little creatures that went around helping fish and shells which got into scrapes. Well, for his part, he would be ashamed to be helped by little, soft creatures that did not even have a shell on their backs. He had lived long enough in the world to know how to take care of himself.

He was a conceited fellow, the old lobster, and not very civil to Tom; and you will hear how he had to change his mind before he was done, as conceited people generally have to. But he was so funny, and Tom was so lonely, that he could not quarrel with him, and they used to sit in holes in the rocks and chat for hours.

About this time Tom had a very strange and important adventure, so important, indeed, that he was very near never finding the water-babies at all;

and I am sure you would have been sorry, too, if that happened.

I hope that you have not forgotten the pretty little girl from Harthover House all this while. At least, here she comes, looking a clean, good little darling, as she always was and always will be.

It befell in the usual short December days that Sir John, hunting all day, and dining at five, fell asleep every evening, and snored so terribly that all the windows in Harthover shook, and the soot fell down the chimneys. Whereon My Lady, being no more able to get conversation out of him than a song out of a dead nightingale, determined to go away and leave him, and the doctor, and Captain Swinger, the agent, to snore together every evening to their hearts' content. So she started for the coast with all her children in order to put herself and them into condition by mild applications of sea water, as was the fashion in those days.

But where she went to nobody must know for fear young children might imagine there are water-babies there, and go to hunt and chase after them.

Now it befell that, on the very shore and over the very rocks where Tom was sitting with his friend the lobster, the little girl, Ellie herself, came walking one day with a very wise man, indeed, called Professor

Ptthmllnsprts.

He had met Sir John at Scarborough, or Fleetwood, or somewhere or other (if you don't care where, nobody else does), and had become friendly with him, and grew very fond of his son and daughter.

So Ellie and he were walking on the rocks, and he was showing her about one in ten thousand of all the beautiful and curious things which are to be seen there. But little Ellie was not satisfied with them at all. She liked much better to play with live children, or even with dolls, which she could pretend were alive; and at last she said in honesty, "I don't care about all these things, because they can't play with me or talk to me. If there were little children in the water now, as there used to be, and I could see them, I would like that."

"Children in the water, you strange little duck?" said the professor.

"Yes," said Ellie. "I know there used to be children in the water, and mermaids too, and mermen. I saw them all in a picture at home. It hangs on the great staircase, and I have looked at it ever since I was a baby and dreamt about it a hundred times; and it is so beautiful that it must be true."

Ah, you dear little Ellie, fresh out of heaven, when

will people understand that one of the deepest and wisest speeches which came out of a human mouth is that: "It is so beautiful that it must be true."

But the professor was not in the least of that opinion.

So he gave her a succinct compendium of his famous paper against water-babies, which had been read at the British Association.

Now little Ellie was, I suppose, a stupid little girl; for, instead of being convinced by Professor Ptthmllnsprts' arguments, she only asked the same question over again.

"But why are there no water-babies?"

I trust and hope that it was because the professor at that moment stepped on the edge of a very sharp mussel and hurt one of his corns that he answered quite sharply:

"Because there ain't!"

Which was not even good English.

And he groped under the weeds so violently with his net that, as it befell, he caught poor little Tom.

He felt the net get very heavy and lifted it out quickly, with Tom all entangled in the meshes.

"Dear me!" he cried, "it has real eyes! Why, it certainly must be a cephalopod! This is most extraordinary."

"No I ain't!" cried Tom as loud as he could, for he did not like to be called bad names.

"It is a water-baby!" cried Ellie; and, of course, it was.

"Water-fiddlesticks, my dear!" said the professor, and he turned away sharply.

There was no denying it. It was a water-baby, and he had said a moment ago that there were none. What was he to do?

Now, if the professor had said to Ellie, "Yes, my darling, it is a water-baby, and a very wonderful thing it is, and it shows how little I know of the wonders of nature in spite of forty years' of deep study." I think that, if the professor had said that, little Ellie would have believed him more, and respected him more, and loved him better than ever she had done up till then. But he held to his opinion stubbornly. So he turned back and poked Tom with his finger for want of anything better to do, and said carelessly: "My dear little maid, you must have dreamt of water-babies last night, your head is so full of them."

Now Tom had been in the most horrible and unspeakable fright all the while and had kept as quiet as he could, for it was fixed in his little head that if a man with clothes on caught him, he might put clothes on him too, and make a dirty chimney sweep of him again. But when the professor poked him, it was more than he could bear, and, between fright and rage, he turned to bay as valiantly as a mouse in a corner, and bit the professor's finger till it began to bleed.

"Oh! ah! yah!" cried he, and glad of an excuse to be rid of Tom, dropped him in the seaweed, from which he dived into the water and was gone in a moment.

"But it was a water-baby, and I heard it speak!" cried Ellie. "Ah, it is gone!" And she jumped down the rock to try to catch Tom before he slipped into the sea.

Too late! What was worse, as she sprang down, she slipped and fell some six feet, hitting her head on a sharp rock; then she lay still.

The professor picked her up and tried to waken her, and called to her, and cried over her, for he loved her very much; but she would not waken at all. So he took her up in his arms and carried her to her governess, and they all went home; and little Ellie was put to bed, and lay there without moving, only now and then waking up and calling out about the water-baby; but no one knew what she meant, and the professor did not tell, for he was ashamed of the way he had behaved.

And, after a week, one moonlight night, the fairies came flying in at the window and brought Ellie such a pretty pair of wings that she could not help putting them on; and she flew with them out of the window and over the land, and over the sea, and up through the clouds, and nobody heard or saw anything of her for a very long while.

And this is why they say that no one had ever seen a water-baby. For my part, I believe that the naturalists get dozens of them when they are out dredging; but they say nothing about them, and throw them overboard again, for fear of spoiling their theories.

CHAPTER FIVE

WITH THE OTHER WATER-BABIES

But what became of little Tom?

He slipped away off the rocks into the water, as I said before. But he could not help thinking of little Ellie. He did not remember who she was, but he knew that she was a little girl, though she was a hundred times as big as he. That is not surprising: size has nothing to do with kindred. So Tom knew that Ellie was a little girl, and thought about her all that day, and longed to have had her to play with; but he had to think of something else very soon.

He was going along the rocks in three fathoms of water, watching the pollock catch prawns, and the wrasses nibble barnacles, shells and all, off the rocks, when he saw a round cage of green twigs, and inside it, looking very much ashamed of himself, sat his friend the lobster, twiddling his horns in place of thumbs.

"What, have you been naughty, and have they put

you in the lock-up?" asked Tom.

The lobster felt a little indignant at such a notion, but he was too much depressed in spirits to argue. So he only said, "I can't get out."

"Why did you get in?"

"After that nasty piece of dead fish." He had thought it looked and smelled very nice when he was outside, and so it did, for a lobster; but now he turned round and abused it because he was angry with himself.

"Where did you get in?"

"Through that round hole at the top."

"Then why don't you get out through it?"

"Because I can't." The lobster twiddled his horns more fiercely than ever, but he was forced to confess.

"I have jumped every which way it is possible at least four thousand times, and I can't get out. I always get underneath one spot and can't find the hole."

Tom looked at the trap, and having more wit than the lobster, he saw plainly what was the matter, as you may if you will look at a lobster pot.

"Wait a bit," said Tom. "Turn your tail up to me, and I'll pull you through hind foremost, and then you won't stick in the spikes."

But the lobster was so stupid and clumsy that he

couldn't locate the hole. Like a great many fox hunters, he was very sharp as long as he was in his own territory, but as soon as they get out of it, they lose their heads; and so the lobster, so to speak, lost his tail.

Tom reached and clawed into the hole after him till he caught hold of him; and then, as was to be expected, the clumsy lobster pulled Tom in head foremost.

"Hullo! this is a fine fix," said Tom. "Come on, use your big claws to break the points off those spikes, and then we shall both get out easily."

"Dear me, I never thought of that," said the lobster, "and after all the experience of life that I have had!"

But they had not broken off half the spikes when they saw a large dark cloud over them. Lo and behold! It was the otter.

How she did grin and grin when she saw Tom. "Yar!" said she, "you little meddlesome wretch, I have you now! I will get you for telling the salmon where I was!" And she crawled all over the pot to reach him.

Tom was horribly frightened, and still more so when she found the hole in the top and began to squeeze herself right down through it, all eyes and teeth. But no sooner was her head inside than the valiant lobster caught her by the nose and held on.

And there they were, all three in the pot, tightly packed and rolling over and over. And the lobster tore at the otter, and the otter tore at the lobster, and both squeezed and thumped poor Tom till he had no breath left in his body; and I don't know what would have happened to him if he had not at last climbed on the otter's back and safely out of the hole.

He was glad to be out, but he would not desert the friend who had saved him; and the first time he saw the lobster's tail uppermost, he caught hold of it and pulled with all his might.

But the lobster would not let go.

"Come on," said Tom; "don't you see she is dead?" And so she was, without any question at all.

And that was the end of the wicked otter.

But the lobster would not let go.

"Come along, you stupid old stick-in-the-mud," cried Tom, "or the fisherman will catch you!" And that was true, for Tom felt someone above beginning to haul up the pot.

But the lobster would not let go.

Tom saw the fisherman haul him up to the side of the boat and thought it was all up with him. But when the lobster saw the fisherman, he gave such a furious and tremendous snap that he snapped out of his hand, and out of the pot, and safe into the sea. But he left his knobbed claw behind him, for it never came into his stupid head to let go, so he just shook his claw off as the easier method. It was something like a bull terrier refusing to let go no matter what, though we know this is not always the brave thing that it seems to be.

Tom asked the lobster why he never thought of letting go. He said very determinedly that it was a point of principle among lobsters. And so it is, as the Mayor of Plymouth found out once to his cost, eight or nine hundred years ago, of course, for if it had happened lately, it would certainly not be kind to mention it.

One day he was so tired of sitting on a hard chair in a grand furred gown, with a gold chain round his neck, hearing one policeman after another come in and sing, "What shall we do with the drunken sailor, so early in the morning?" and answering them each exactly alike:

"Put him in the round house till he gets sober, so early in the morning."

When it was over, he jumped up and played leap frog with the town clerk till he burst his buttons, and then had his luncheon, and burst some more buttons, and then said, "It is a low spring tide. I shall go out this afternoon and cut my capers."

What the mayor meant was that he would go and have an afternoon's fun, like any schoolboy, and catch lobsters with an iron hook.

So to the Mewstone he went, and for lobsters he looked. And when he came to a certain crack in the rocks he was so excited that, instead of putting in his hook, he put in his hand; and a lobster was at home and caught him by the finger and held on.

"Yah!" said the mayor, and pulled as hard as he dared; but the more he pulled, the more the lobster pinched, till he was forced to stop.

Then he tried to get his hook in with his other hand, but the hole was too narrow.

Then he pulled again, but he could not stand the pain.

Then he shouted and bawled for help, but there was no one nearer him than the men-of-war inside the breakwater.

Then he began to turn a little pale, for the tide flowed and still the lobster held on.

Then he turned quite white, for the tide was up to his knees and still the lobster held on.

Then he thought of cutting off his finger, but he needed two things to do it with: courage and a knife, and he didn't have either.

Then he turned quite yellow, for the tide was up to his waist and still the lobster held on.

Then he thought over all the naughty things he had ever done: all the sand which he had put in the sugar, and the sloe leaves in the tea, and the water in the honey, and the salt in the tobacco (because his brother was a brewer, and a man must help his own kin).

Then he turned quite blue, for the tide was up to his breast and still the lobster held on.

And then he turned all hues at once, and raised his eyes like a duck in thunder, for the water was up to his chin and still the lobster held on.

And then came a man-of-war's boat round the Mewstone and saw his head sticking up out of the water. One said it was a keg of brandy, and another that it was a coconut, and another that it was a loose buoy, and another that it was a thieving diver, and wanted to fire at it, which would not have been pleasant for the mayor. But just then such a yell came out of a great hole in the middle of it that the midshipman in charge guessed what it was and ordered them pull up to it as fast as they could. So somehow or other the sailors got the lobster away, and set the mayor free. He never went lobster-catching again; and we will hope he put no more salt in the tobacco, not even to sell his brother's beer.

And that is the story of the Mayor of Plymouth, which has two advantages: first, that of being true, and second, that of having (as folks say all good stories ought to have) no moral whatsoever. Nor has any part of this book, because it is a fairy tale.

And now a most wonderful thing happened to Tom, for he had not left the lobster five minutes before he came upon a water-baby.

It was a real live water-baby, sitting on the white sand and working busily on a little point of rock. When it saw Tom, it looked up for a moment and then cried, "Why, you are a new baby. Oh, how very delightful!"

And it ran to Tom, and Tom ran to it, and they hugged and kissed each other for ever so long. For they did not need any formal introductions there under the water.

At last Tom said, "Oh, where have you been all this while? I have been looking for you so long, and I have been so lonely."

"We have been here for days and days. There are hundreds of us near the rocks. How is it you did not see us, or hear us when we sing and romp every evening before we go home?"

He swam onto the buoy and looked around for water-babies; but there were none to be seen (page 120)

He used to come out in the night and sit upon a point of rock
(page 125)

Tom looked at the baby again, and then he said happily:

"Well, this is wonderful. I have seen things just like you again and again, but I thought you were shells or sea creatures. I never took you for water-babies like myself."

"Now," said the baby, "come and help me, or I shall not have finished before my brothers and sisters come and it is time to go home."

"What shall I help you at?"

"Look at this poor, dear, little rock. A big, clumsy boulder came rolling by in the last storm and knocked its head all off, and rubbed off all its flowers. And now I must plant it again with seaweeds and coralline and anemones, and I will make it the prettiest little rock garden on all the shore."

So they worked away at the rock, and planted it, and smoothed the sand down round it, and they had great fun till the tide began to turn. And then Tom heard all the other babies coming, laughing and singing and shouting and romping; and the noise they made was just like the noise of the ripple. So he knew that he had been hearing and seeing the water-babies all along, only he did not know them because his eyes and ears were not opened.

And in they came, dozens and dozens of them,

some bigger than Tom and some smaller, all in the neatest little white bathing suits; and when they found that he was a new baby, they hugged him and kissed him, and then put him in the middle and danced round him on the sand, and there was no one ever so happy as poor little Tom.

"Now then," they cried all at once, "we must go home, we must go home, or the tide will leave us stranded. We have mended all the broken seaweed, and put all the rock pools in order, and planted all the shells in the sand again, and nobody will see where the ugly storm swept in last week."

And this is the reason why the rock pools are always so neat and clean, because the water-babies come inshore after every storm to sweep them out, and comb them down, and put them all to rights again.

And where is the home of the water-babies? In St. Brandan's fairy isle.

Did you never hear of the blessed St. Brandan, how he preached to the Irish on the wild, wild Kerry coast, he and five other hermits, till they were weary and longed to rest? For the Irish would not listen to them.

So St. Brandan went out to the point of Old Dunmore and looked over the tideway roaring round the Blasquets at the end of all the world and away into the ocean, and sighed, "Ah, that I had wings as a dove!" And far away he saw a blue fairy sea, and golden fairy islands, and he said, "Those are the islands of the blessed." Then he and his friends got into a fishing boat and sailed away and away to the west, and were never heard of more.

And when St. Brandan and the hermits came to that fairy isle, they found it overgrown with cedars and full of beautiful birds. And he sat down under the cedars and preached to all the birds in the air. And they liked his sermons so well that they told the fish in the sea. And they came and St. Brandan preached to them, and the fish told the water-babies, who live in the caves under the isle. And they came up by hundreds every Sunday, and St. Brandan started a neat little Sunday school. And there he taught the water-babies for many hundreds of years, till his eyes grew too dim to see and his beard grew so long that he dared not walk for fear of treading on it, which might have made him go tumbling down. And at last he and the five hermits fell fast asleep under the cedar trees, and there they sleep unto this day. But the fairies took the water-babies under their protective wings, and taught them their lessons themselves.

Now, when Tom got there he found that the isle stood on pillars, and that its roots were full of caves. There were pillars of black basalt, like Staffa, and pillars of green and crimson serpentine, like Kynance; and pillars ribboned with red and white and yellow sandstone, like Livermead; and there were blue grottoes like Capri, and white grottoes like Adelsberg; all curtained and draped with seaweeds, purple and crimson, green and brown, and strewn with soft white sand on which the water-babies sleep every night.

But, to keep the place clean and sweet, the crabs picked up all the scraps off the floor and ate them like so many monkeys, while the rocks were covered with ten thousand sea anemones and corals and madrepores, who scavenged the water all day long and kept it nice and pure. But, to make up to them for having to do such nasty work, they were not left gritty and dirty as poor chimney sweeps are. No. The fairies are more considerate and just than that, and have dressed them all in the most beautiful shades and patterns, till they look like vast flowerbeds of gay blossoms.

And, instead of guards and police to keep out nasty things at night, there were thousands and thousands of water snakes, and most wonderful creatures they were. They were dressed in green velvet and black velvet and purple velvet, and were jointed in rings, and some of them had three hundred brains apiece so that they must have been uncommonly shrewd detectives; and some had eyes in their tails; and some had eyes in every joint so that they kept a very sharp lookout; and when they wanted a baby snake, they just grew one at the end of their own tails, and when it was able to take care of itself, it dropped off so that they brought up their families very cheaply.

But if any nasty thing came by, out they rushed upon it, and then out of each of their hundreds of feet there sprang a whole load of

Scythes, Pickaxes,
Penknives, Rapiers,
Sabres, Creeses,
Swords, Javelins,
Lances, Halberts,
Poleaxes, Fishhooks,
Corkscrews, Pins, and Needles

which stabbed, shot, poked, pricked, scratched, ripped, pinked, and crimped those naughty beasts so terribly that they had to run for their lives, or else be chopped into small pieces and be eaten up. And, if that is not all true, every word, then there is no faith in microscopes and all is over with science.

And there were the water-babies in thousands, more than Tom, or you either, could count. All the little children whom the good fairies love because their cruel mothers and fathers will not; all who are untaught and brought up without care; all who come to grief by ill usage or ignorance or neglect; all the little children who are given gin when they are young, or are allowed to drink out of hot kettles, or to fall into the fire; all the children in alleys and courts and tumbledown cottages, who die of fever, and cholera, and measles, and scarlatina, and nasty complaints which no one has any business to have, and which no one will have some day, when folk have common sense; and all the little children who have been killed by cruel masters and wicked soldiers fighting in wars.

But I wish Tom had given up all his naughty tricks, and left off tormenting dumb animals now that he had plenty of playmates to amuse him. Instead of that, I am sorry to say, he went on bothering the creatures, all but the water snakes, for they would stand no nonsense. So he tickled the madrepores to make them shut up, and frightened the crabs to make them hide in the sand and peep out at him with the tips of their eyes; and put stones into the anemones' mouths to make them fancy that their dinner was coming when, in fact, it wasn't!

The other children warned him and said, "Take care what you do. Mrs. Bedonebyasyoudid is coming." But Tom never heeded them, being riotous with high spirits and good luck, till, one early Friday morning, Mrs. Bedonebyasyoudid did come along.

A very huge woman she was; and when the children saw her, they all stood in a row, very straight, and smoothed down their clothes, and folded their hands and put them behind them, just as if they were going to be examined by the inspector.

She had on a black bonnet and a black shawl, and no crinoline at all, and a pair of large green spectacles. She had a large hooked nose, hooked so much that the bridge of it stood up above her eyebrows; and under her arm she carried a long birch rod. Indeed, she was so ugly that Tom was tempted to make faces at her, but did not; for he did not like the look of the birch rod under her arm.

She looked at the children one by one and seemed very much pleased with them, though she never asked them one question about how they were behaving; and then she began giving them all sorts of nice sea-things: sea-cakes, sea-apples, sea-oranges, sea-bullseyes, sea-toffee; and to the very best of all she gave sea-ices, made out of sea-cows' cream, which never melt underwater.

Now, little Tom watched all these sweet thing being given away till his mouth watered and his eyes grew as round as an owl's. He hoped and hoped that his turn would come at last; and so it did. For finally the woman called him up, and held out her fingers with something in them, and popped it into his mouth; but it was a nasty, cold, hard pebble!

"You are a very cruel woman," said he, and began to whimper.

"And you are a very cruel boy, who puts pebbles into the sea anemones' mouths for them to take in and make them think that they had caught a good dinner! As you did to them, so I am doing to you."

"I did not know there was any harm in it," said Tom.

"Then you know now. People continually say that to me. But I tell them, if you don't know that fire burns, that is no reason that it should not burn you. And so, if you do not know that things are wrong, that is no reason why you should not be punished for them, though not as much, not as much, my little man as if you did know." (And the lady looked very kindly, after all.)

"Well, you are a little hard on a poor lad," said Tom.

"Not at all. I am the best friend you ever had in all your life. But I tell you I cannot help punishing people when they do wrong. I like it no more than they do. I am often very, very sorry for them, poor things, but I cannot help it. If I tried not to do it, I would do it all the same. For I work by machinery, just like an engine, and am full of wheels and springs inside, and am wound up very carefully so that I cannot help going."

"Was it a long time ago that they wound you up?" asked Tom. For he thought cunningly. "She will run down some day, or they may forget to wind her up, as Grimes used to forget to wind his watch when he came from the public house; and then I shall be safe."

"I was wound up once and for all, so long ago that I forgot all about it."

"Dear me," said Tom, "you must have been made a long time!"

"I never was made, my child, and I shall go forever and ever, for I am as old as Eternity, and yet as young as Time."

And then there came over the woman's face a very curious expression, very solemn, and very sad, and yet very, very sweet. And she looked up and away, as if she were gazing through the sea and through the sky at something far, far off; and as she did so there came such a quiet, tender, patient, hopeful smile over her face that Tom thought for the moment that she did not look ugly at all. And, indeed, she did not. For she was like a great many people who do not have a pretty feature in their faces and yet are lovely to behold, and draw little children's hearts to them at once, because though the house is plain as plain, yet from the windows a beautiful and good spirit is looking forth.

And Tom smiled in her face as she looked so pleasant for the moment. And the strange fairy smiled too, and said:

"Yes. You thought me very ugly just now, did you not?"

Tom hung down his head, and his ears got very red with shame.

"And I am very ugly. I am the ugliest fairy in the world, and I shall be till people behave themselves as they ought to do. And then I shall grow as handsome as my sister, who is the loveliest fairy in the world, and her name is Mrs. Doasyouwouldbedoneby. So she begins where I end, and I begin where she ends, and those who will not listen to her must listen to me, as you will see. Now, all of you run away except Tom, who may stay and see what I am going to do. It will be a very good warning for him before he goes to school.

"Now, Tom, every Friday I come and call up all who have been nasty to little children, and treat them as they treated the children."

At that Tom was frightened and crept under a stone, which made the two crabs who lived there very angry, and frightened their friend, the butterfish, into flapping hysterics; but he would not move for them.

Then she called up all the careless nurserymaids, and stuck pins into them all over, and wheeled them around in perambulators with tight straps across their stomachs and their heads and arms hanging over the side, till they were quite sick and dull, and would have had sunstrokes except that, being under the water, they could only have waterstrokes. This, I assure you is nearly as bad, as you will find if you try to sit under a mill wheel. And listen. When you hear a rumbling at the bottom of the sea, sailors will tell you that it is a groundswell, but now you know better. It is the fairy wheeling the maids around in perambulators.

And by that time she was so tired, she had to go to lunch.

After lunch she set to work again, and called up all the cruel schoolmasters, whole regiments and brigades of them; and when she saw them, she frowned most terribly, and set to work in earnest, as if the best part of the day's work were to come. More than half of them were nasty, dirty, frowzy, grubby, smelly old men, who, because they dared not hit a person of their own size, amused themselves with beating little children instead.

She boxed their ears and thumped them over the head with rulers, and pandied their hands with canes, and told them that they told stories, and were this and that bad sort of people; and the more they were very indignant, and declared their innocence, and swore they told the truth, the more she declared they were not, and that they were only telling lies; and at last she beat them all soundly with her great birch rod and set them each the task of three hundred thousand lines of Hebrew to learn by heart before she came back next Friday.

At that they all cried and howled so that their breaths came up through the sea like bubbles out of soda water; and that is one reason for the bubbles in the sea. There are others, but that is the one which principally concerns little boys. And by this time she was so tired that she was glad to stop; and, indeed, she had done a very good day's work.

Tom did not entirely dislike this fairy, but he could

not help thinking her a little spiteful; and no wonder if she were, poor old soul, for if she has to wait to grow handsome till people do as they would be done by, she knows very well that she will have to wait a very long time.

Tom longed to ask her one question, and, after all, whenever she looked at him she seemed to change her expression entirely, and she did not look cross at all. Now and then there was a funny smile on her face, and she chuckled to herself in a way which gave Tom courage, and at last he said:

"Pray, ma'am, may I ask you a question?"

"Certainly, my little dear."

"Why don't you bring all the bad masters here and punish them well too? The butties that knock about the poor collier boys; and the nailers that file off their lads' noses and hammer their fingers; and all the master sweeps, like my master Grimes? I saw him fall into the water long ago, so I expected he would surely have been here. I can tell you he was very bad to me."

Then the fairy looked so very stern that Tom was frightened, and sorry that he had been so bold. But she was not angry with him. She only answered, "I look after them all the week round, and they are in a very different place from this, because they well knew that they were doing wrong.

"But these people," she went on, "did not know that they were doing wrong. They were only stupid and impatient; and, therefore, I only punish them till they become patient and learn to use their common sense like reasonable beings. And now, you be a good boy and do as you would be done by, which they did not; and then, when my sister, Mrs. Doasyouwouldbedoneby, comes on Sunday, perhaps she will take notice of you, and teach you how to behave. She understands that better than I do."

And then she went away.

Tom was very glad to hear that there was no chance of meeting Grimes again, though he was a little sorry for him, considering that he used sometimes to give him the leavings of the beer. But he determined to be a very good boy all Saturday, and he was; for he never frightened one crab, or tickled any live corals, or put stones into the sea anemones' mouths to make them think they had caught some dinner. And when Sunday morning came, sure enough, Mrs. Doasyouwouldbedoneby appeared. At this, all the little water-babies began dancing and clapping their hands, and Tom danced along with all his might.

And as for the pretty fairy, I cannot tell you what

the shade of her hair was, or of her eyes. Nor could Tom. For, when anyone looks at her, all they can think of is that she has the sweetest, kindest, tenderest, funniest, merriest face they ever saw, or want to see. Tom saw that she was a very tall woman, as tall as her sister; but instead of being gnarly, and horny, and scaly, and prickly like her, she was the nicest,

softest,

smoothest,

plumpest,

most cuddly,

lovable and delightful creature who ever took care of a baby; and she understood babies thoroughly, for she had plenty of her own, whole rows and regiments of them, and has to this day. And all her delight, whenever she had a spare moment, was to play with babies, in which she showed herself a woman of sense; for babies are the best company, and the pleasantest playmates in the world.

At least, so all the wise people in the world think. And, therefore, when the children saw her, they naturally all caught hold of her, and pulled her along, till she sat down on a stone, and climbed into her lap, and clung round her neck, and caught hold of her hands; and then they all put their thumbs into their mouths, and began hugging her and purring like so many kittens, as they ought to have done. Those who could not get so near sat down on the sand, and hugged her feet, for no one, you know, wears shoes in the water. And Tom stood staring at them, for he could not understand what it was all about.

"And who are you, you little darling?" she said.

"Oh, that is the new baby!" they all cried, pulling their thumbs out of their mouths, "and he never had any mother," and they all put their thumbs back again, for they did not wish to lose any time.

"Then I will be his mother, and he shall have the very best place; so move away, all of you, this moment."

And she took up two great armfuls of babies, nine hundred under one arm and thirteen hundred under the other, and threw them away, right and left, into the water. But they didn't mind it any more than the naughty boys in Struwelpeter minded when St. Nicholas dipped them in his inkstand. They did not even take their thumbs out of their mouths, but came paddling and wriggling back to her like so many tadpoles, till you could see nothing of her from head to foot for the swarm of little babies.

She took Tom in her arms, and laid him in the

Inside the cage, looking very ashamed of himself, sat the lobster (page 137)

Tom had not left the lobster five minutes before he came upon a water-baby (page 144)

softest place of all, and kissed him, and patted him, and talked to him tenderly and softly, saying such things as he had never heard before in his life; and Tom looked up into her eyes, and loved her, and loved, till he fell fast asleep from the ecstasy of pure love.

When he woke, she was telling the children a story. And what story did she tell them?

One story she told them, which begins every Christmas Eve, and yet never ends at all forever and ever; and, as she went on, the children took their thumbs out of their mouths and listened seriously but not sadly at all, for she never told them anything sad; and Tom listened too, and never grew tired of listening. And he listened so long that he fell fast asleep again, and, when he woke, the fairy was still looking after him.

"Don't go away," said little Tom. "This is so nice. I never had anyone to hug and kiss me before."

"Don't go away," said the children. "You have not sung us one song."

"Well, I have time for only one. So what shall it be?"

"The doll you lost! The doll you lost!" cried all the babies at once.

So the lovely fairy sang:

I once had a sweet little doll, dears,
  The prettiest doll in the world;
Her cheeks were so red and so white, dears,
  And her hair was so charmingly curled.
But I lost my poor little doll, dears,
  As I played in the heath one day;
And I cried for her more than a week, dears,
  But I never could find where she lay.

I found my poor little doll, dears,
  As I played in the heath one day:
Folk say she is terribly changed, dears,
  For her paint is all washed away,
And her arm trodden off by the cows, dears,
  And her hair not the least bit curled:
Yet, for old sakes' sake she is still, dears,
  The prettiest doll in the world.

"Now," said the fairy to Tom, "will you be a good boy for my sake, and stop tormenting sea beasts till I come back?"

"And will you cuddle me again?" said poor little Tom.

"Of course I will, you little duck. I would like to take you with me and cuddle you all the way, only I must not." And away she went – back to where she had come from.

So Tom really tried to be a good boy, and did not torment sea beasts after that as long as he lived; and he is still alive, I assure you.

Oh, how good little boys and girls ought to be who have kind mammas to cuddle them and tell them stories; and how afraid they ought to be of growing naughty, and bringing tears into their mammas' pretty eyes!

CHAPTER SIX

TOM AND ELLIE

Now you may think that Tom was very good when he had everything that he could want or wish for, but you would be very much mistaken. For he grew so fond of the sea-bullseyes and sea-lollipops that his foolish little head could think of nothing else, and he was always longing for more, and wondering when the dear fairy would come again and give him some, and what she would give him, and how much, and whether she would give him more than the others. And he thought of nothing but lollipops by day, and dreamt of nothing else by night. And what happened then?

Well, he began to watch the fairy to see where she kept the sweet things, and he began hiding, and sneaking, and following her, and pretending to be looking the other way or going after something else, till he found out that she kept them in a beautiful mother-of-pearl cabinet away in a deep crack of the rocks.

And he longed to go to the cabinet, and yet he was afraid; and then he longed again, and was less afraid; and at last, by continual thinking about it, he longed so violently that he was not afraid at all. And one night, when all the other water-babies were asleep, and he could not sleep for thinking of lollipops, he crept away among the rocks and got to the cabinet, and behold! It was open.

But, when he saw all the nice things inside, instead of being delighted, he was very frightened and wished he had never come there. But he thought he would only touch them, and he did; and then he would only taste one, and he did; and then he would only eat one, and he did; and then he would only eat two, and then three, and so on; and then he was terrified that he might be caught and began gobbling them down so fast that he did not taste them or have any pleasure in them; and then he felt sick and decided to have only one more; and then only one more, till he had eaten them all up.

And all the while, close behind him, stood Mrs. Bedonebyasyoudid. Some people may say, "But why did she not keep her cupboard locked?" Well, I know. It may seem a very strange thing, but she never keeps her cupboard locked; everyone may go and taste for themselves, and take the consequences.

It is very odd, but it is so, and I am sure she knows best. Perhaps she wants people to keep their fingers out of the fire by having them burned.

She took off her spectacles, because she did not like to see too much; and in her pity she arched up her eyebrows all the way into her hair, and her eyes grew so wide that they could have taken in all the sorrows of the world, and filled with great big tears.

But all she said was:

"Ah, you poor little dear! You are just like all the rest."

But she said it to herself so that Tom neither heard nor saw her. Now, you must not imagine that she was at all sentimental. If you think that she is going to let you, or me, or any human being off when we do wrong, just because she is too tender-hearted to punish us, then you will find that you are very much mistaken, as many a person learns every day and every year.

But what did the fairy do when she saw that all her lollipops were eaten?

Did she fly at Tom, catch him by the scruff of the neck,

hold him,

hump him,

hurry him,

hit him,
poke him,
pull him,
pinch him,
push him,
pound him,
put him in the corner,
shake him,
slap him,
set him on a cold stone to make him sorry, and so forth?

Not a bit. You may watch her at work if you know where to find her. But you will never see her do that. For, if she had, she knew very well that Tom would have fought, and kicked, and bit, and said bad words, and turned once more that moment into a naughty, wild little chimney sweep, with his hand, like Ishmael's in the Bible story, against every person, and every person's hand against him.

Did she question him, hurry him, frighten him, threaten him, to make him confess? Not a bit. For, if she had, she would have tempted him to tell lies in his fright, and that would have been worse for him, if possible, than becoming an overworked chimney sweep again.

She just said nothing at all about the matter, not

even when Tom came the next day with the rest for sweet things. He was horribly afraid of coming, but he was still more afraid of staying away, which might make the others suspect him. He was dreadfully afraid that there would be no sweets because he had eaten them all, and that the fairy would try to find out who had taken them. But, behold! She pulled out as many as ever, which astonished Tom and frightened him still more.

And, when the fairy looked him full in the face, he shook from head to foot. However, she gave him his share like the rest, and he thought to himself that she could not have found out what he had done.

But, when he put the sweets into his mouth, he hated the taste of them, and they made him so sick that he had to get away as fast as he could; and terribly sick he was, and very cross and unhappy all the week after.

Then, when next week came, he got his share again, and again the fairy looked him full in the face, but more sadly than she had ever looked. And he could not bear the sweets, but took them again in spite of himself.

And when Mrs. Doasyouwouldbedoneby came, he wanted to be cuddled like the rest, but she said very seriously:

"I would like to hug you, but I cannot, for you are so horny and prickly."

And when Tom looked at himself, he saw that he was as prickly as a sea-egg.

Which was quite natural; for you must know and believe that people's souls make their bodies just as a snail makes its shell. (I am not joking, little children. I am in serious, solemn earnest.) And therefore, when Tom's soul grew all prickly with naughty deeds and tempers, his body could not help growing prickly too, so that nobody would cuddle him, or play with him, or even like to look at him.

What could Tom do now but go away, and hide in a corner and cry? For nobody would play with him, and he knew exactly why.

He was so miserable all that week that when the ugly fairy came and looked at him full in the face once more, more seriously and sadly than ever, he could stand it no longer. He pushed the sweetmeats away, saying "No, I don't want any. I can't bear them now," and then burst out crying, poor little man, and told Mrs. Bedonebyasyoudid everything just as it had happened.

He was horribly frightened when he had finished, for he expected her to punish him very severely. But, instead, she picked him up and kissed him, which was not exactly pleasant, for her chin was very bristly indeed; but he was so lonely-hearted, he thought her rough kiss was better than none.

"I will forgive you, little man," she said. "I always forgive everyone the moment they tell me the truth of their own accord."

"Then you will take away all these nasty prickles?" asked Tom.

"That is a very different matter. You put them there yourself, and only you can take them away."

"But how can I do that?" asked Tom, crying afresh.

"Well, I think it is time for you to go to school, so I shall bring a schoolmistress who will teach you how to get rid of your prickles." And then, suddenly, she went away.

Tom was frightened at the notion of a schoolmistress, for he thought she would certainly come with a birch rod or a cane; but he comforted himself, at last, that she might be something like the old woman in Vendale. This she was not in the least, for, when the fairy brought her, she was the most beautiful little girl that ever was seen, with long curls floating behind her like a golden cloud, and long robes floating all round her like a silver cloud.

"There he is," said the fairy. You must teach him to be good, whether you like it or not."

"I know," said the little girl; but she did not seem to like it, for she put her finger in her mouth and looked at Tom under her brows; and Tom put his finger in his mouth and looked at her under his brows, for he was horribly ashamed of himself.

The little girl seemed hardly to know how to begin, and perhaps she would never have begun at all if poor Tom had not burst out crying, and begged her to teach him to be good and help him to get rid of the prickles; and at that she began teaching him as tender-heartedly as ever a child was taught in the world.

And what did the little girl teach Tom? She taught him, first, what you have been taught ever since you said your first prayers at your mother's knee; but she taught him much more simply. For the lessons in that world, my child, have no such hard words in them like the lessons in this world do.

She taught Tom every day in the week except that on Sundays she always went away, and the kind fairy took her place. And before she had taught Tom many Sundays, his prickles had vanished completely and his skin was smooth and clean again.

"Dear me!" said the little girl. "Why, I know you now. You are the very same little chimney sweep who came into my bedroom."

"Dear me!" cried Tom. "And I know you too. You are the very little girl all in white whom I saw in bed." And he longed to hug and kiss her, but did not because he remembered that she was a lady born. So he only jumped round and round her till he grew very very tired.

And then they began telling each other their whole story: how he had jumped into the water, and she had fallen over the rock; how he had swum down to the sea, and how she had flown out of the window; how this; that, and the other, till it was all talked out; and then they both began over again, and I can't say which of the two talked fastest.

Then they set to work at their lessons again, and both liked them so well that they went on with them till seven full years were past and gone.

You may imagine that Tom was content and happy all those seven years, but the truth is, he was not. He always had one thing on his mind, and that was where little Ellie went to on Sundays.

To a very beautiful place, she said.

But what was the beautiful place like, and where was it?

Ah, that is just what she could not say. And it is strange, but true, that no one can say, and that those who have been in it most often, or even nearest to it, can say least about it, and make people understand least what it is like. There are a good many folk in the Other-end-of-Nowhere (where Tom went later), who pretend to know it from north to south as well as if they had been postmen there; but, as they are safe at the Other-end-of-Nowhere, nine hundred and ninety-nine million miles away, what they say cannot concern us.

But the dear, sweet, loving, wise, good, self-sacrificing people who really go there, can never tell you anything about it, except that is is the most beautiful place in all the world; and, if you ask them more, they grow modest, and hold their peace for fear of being laughed at; and right they are. All that good little Ellie could say was that it was worth all the rest of the world put together. And, of course, that only made Tom the more anxious to go there too.

"Dear Ellie," he said at last, "I must know why I cannot go with you to that wonderful place on Sundays, or I shall have no peace and give you none."

"You must ask the fairies that."

So when Mrs. Bedonebyasyoudid next came, Tom asked her.

"Little boys who are only fit to play with sea beasts cannot go there," she said. "Those who go there must first go where they do not like, and do what they do not like, and help somebody they do not like."

"Did Ellie do that?"

"Ask her."

And Ellie blushed, and said, "Yes, Tom. I did not like coming here at first. I was so much happier at home, where it is always Sunday. And I was afraid of you, Tom, at first, because . . . because . . . "

"Because I was so full of prickles? But I am not prickly now, am I?"

"No," said Ellie. "I like you very much now, and I like coming here too."

"And perhaps," said the fairy to Tom, "you will learn to like going where you don't like, the same way Ellie has."

Tom was very unhappy at that. And, when Ellie went away on Sunday, he fretted and cried all day, and did not want to listen to the fairy's stories about good children, though they were better stories than ever. Indeed, the more he heard of them, the less he liked to listen, because they were all about children who did what they did not like, and took trouble for other people, and worked to feed their little brothers and sisters instead of only wanting to play. And, when she began to tell a story about a holy child in old times, who was killed because it would not worship idols, Tom could bear no more, and ran away and hid among the rocks.

And, when Ellie came back, he was shy with her because he imagined she looked down on him, and thought him a coward. And then he grew cross with her, because she was superior to him and did what he could not do. And poor Ellie was surprised and sad; and at last Tom burst out crying, but he would not tell her what was really in his mind. And all the while he was eaten up with curiosity to know where Ellie went to so that he began to get dissatisfied with his playmates and the sea palace and everything else. But perhaps that made matters all the easier for him; for he grew so discontened with everything around him that he did not want to stay, and did not care where he went.

"Well," he said at last. "I am so miserable here, I'll go. Will you go with me?"

"Ah!" said Ellie, "I wish I could, but the worst of it is that the fairy says you must go alone, if you go at all. Now don't poke that poor crab, Tom" (for he was feeling very naughty and mischievious), "or the fairy will have to punish you."

Tom was very near saying, "I don't care if she does," but he stopped himself in time.

"I know what she wants me to do," he said,

All her delight, whenever she had a spare moment, was to play with babies (page 161)

"I would like to hug you, but I cannot for you are so horny and prickly" (page 174)

whimpering most dolefully. "She wants me to go after that horrid old Grimes. I don't like him, that's certain. And if I find him, he will turn me into a chimney sweep again, I know. That's what I have been afraid of all along."

"No, he won't. I know as much as that. Nobody can turn water-babies into sweeps, or hurt them at all, as long as they are good."

"Ah!" said naughty Tom, "I see what you want. You are trying to get me to go away because you are tired of me and want to get rid of me."

Little Ellie opened her eyes very wide at that, and they were all brimming over with tears.

"Oh, Tom, Tom!" she said, very mournfully. Then she cried, "Oh, Tom! where are you?"

And Tom cried, "Oh, Ellie, where are you?"

For neither of them could see each other at all. Little Ellie vanished entirely, and Tom heard her voice calling him. But it grew smaller and smaller, and fainter and fainter, till all was silent.

Tom was horribly frightened. He swam up and down among the rocks, into all the halls and chambers, faster than ever he swam before, but could not find her. He shouted after her, but she did not answer. He asked all the other water-babies, but they had not seen her. At last he went up to the top of the water and began crying and screaming for Mrs. Bedonebyasyoudid. This, perhaps, was the best thing to do, for she came in a moment.

"Oh!" said Tom. "Oh dear, oh dear! I have been naughty to Ellie, and I have killed her. I know I have killed her."

"Not quite that," said the fairy; "but I have sent her away, and she will not come back again for I do not know how long." And at that Tom cried so bitterly that the salt sea was swelled with his tears, and the tide was .3,954,620,819 of an inch higher than it had been the day before. Perhaps that was owing to the waxing of the moon. It may have been so, but it is considered right in the new philosophy, you know, to give spiritual causes for physical phenomena, especially at parlour tables; and, of course, physical causes for spiritual ones, like thinking, and praying, and knowing right from wrong. And so they "odds it till it comes even," as folk say in the county of Berkshire.

"How cruel of you to send Ellie away!" sobbed Tom. "I will find her again if I have to go to the world's end to look for her."

The fairy did not slap Tom and tell him to hold his tongue, but took him on her lap very kindly, just as her sister would have done, and explained to him how it was not her fault, because she was wound up inside, like watches, and could not help doing things whether she liked it or not. And then she told him how he had been in the nursery long enough, and must go out and see the world if he intended ever to be a man; and how he must go all alone, as everyone else that ever was born has to do, and see with his own eyes, and smell with his own nose, and make his own bed and lie on it, and burn his own fingers if he foolishly put them into the fire.

Then she told him how many fine things there were to be seen in the world, and what an odd, curious, pleasant, orderly, respectable, well-managed, and, on the whole, successful (as, indeed, might have been expected) sort of a place it was, if people would only be moderately brave and honest and good in it; and then she told him not to be afraid of anything he met, for nothing would harm him if he remembered all his lessons and did what he knew was right. And at last she comforted poor little Tom so much that he was quite eager to go, and wanted to set out that minute. "I only wish," he said, "that I might see Ellie once before I went!"

"Why do you want that?"

"Because, because I should be so much happier if I thought she had forgiven me."

And in the twinkling of an eye, there stood Ellie, smiling, and looking so happy that Tom longed to kiss her, but was still afraid it would not be respectable because she was a lady born.

"I am going, Ellie!" said Tom. "I am going, if it is to the world's end. But I don't like going at all, and that's the truth."

"Pooh! pooh! pooh!" said the fairy. "You will like it very well indeed, you little rogue, and you know that at the bottom of your heart."

CHAPTER SEVEN

TO THE OTHER-END-OF- NOWHERE

Tom said, "Now I am ready to be off, if it's to the world's end."

"Ah!" said the fairy, "that is a brave, good boy. But you must go farther than the world's end if you want to find Mr. Grimes, for he is at the Other-end-of-Nowhere. You must go to Shiny Wall, and through the white gate that never was opened; and then you will come to Peacepool and Mother Carey's Haven, where the good whales go when they die. And there Mother Carey will tell you the way to the Other-end-of-Nowhere, and there you will find Mr. Grimes."

"Oh, dear!" said Tom. "But I do not know my way to Shiny Wall, or even where to begin to find it."

"Little boys must take the trouble to find out things for themselves, or they will never grow to be men. So you must ask all the beasts in the sea and the birds in the air, and if you have been good to them, some of them will tell you the way to Shiny Wall."

"Well," said Tom, "it will be a long journey, so I had better start at once. Good-bye, Ellie. You know I am getting to be a big boy, and must go out and see the world."

"I know you must," said Ellie; "but you will not forget me, Tom. I shall wait here till you come."

And she shook hands with him and said goodbye to him.

So Tom started out and asked all the beasts in the sea, and all the birds in the air, but none of them knew the way to Shiny Wall. Why? He was still too far south.

Then he met a ship, far larger than he had ever seen, a gallant ocean steamer with a long cloud of smoke trailing behind.

Onto the quarterdeck came a very pretty lady in deep, black widows' weeds, with a baby in her arms. She leaned over the quarterdeck, and looked back and back toward England far away, and as she looked she sang:

I

"Soft, soft wind from out the sweet south sliding,
Waft thy silver cloud-webs athwart the summer sea;

Thin, thin threads of mist on dewy fingers twining,
Weave a veil of dappled gauze to shade my babe and me.

II

"Deep, deep Love, within thine own abyss abiding,
Pour Thyself abroad, O Lord, on earth and air and sea;
Worn weary hearts within Thy holy temple hiding,
Shield from sorrow, sin, and shame my helpless babe and me."

Her voice was so soft and low, and the music of the air so sweet that Tom could have listened to it all day. But as she held the baby over the gallery rail to show it the dolphins leaping and the water gurgling in the ship's wake, lo and behold! The baby saw Tom.

He was quite sure of that, for, when their eyes met, the baby smiled and held out his hands; and Tom smiled and held out his hands too; and the baby kicked and leaped, as if it wanted to jump overboard to him.

"What do you see, my darling?" said his mother. And her eyes followed the baby's till she too caught sight of Tom swimming among the foam beads below the surface.

She gave a little start and shriek and then she said quietly, "Babies in the sea? Well, perhaps it is the happiest place for them." Then she waved her hand to Tom and cried, "Wait a bit, darling, only a bit, and perhaps we shall go with you and be at rest."

At that an old nurse, all in black, came out and talked to her and drew her in. And Tom turned away northward, sad and wondering. He watched the great steamer slide away into the dusk, and the lights on board peep out one by one and die out again, and the long bar of smoke fade away into the evening mist, till it was out of sight.

Then he swam north again, day after day, till at last he met the King of the Herrings with a curry comb growing out of his nose, and a sprat in his mouth for a cigar, and asked him the way to Shiny Wall. The king bolted his sprat head foremost and said:

"If I were you, young gentleman, I would go to the Allalonestone and ask the last of the gairfowl. She is of a very ancient clan, very nearly as ancient as my own, and knows a good deal which these modern upstarts don't, as ladies of old houses are likely to do."

Tom asked his way to her and the King of the Herrings told him very kindly, for he was a courteous old gentleman of the old school, though he was horribly ugly, and strangely bedizened too, like the old dandies who lounge in the clubhouse windows.

But just as Tom had thanked him and set off, he called after, "Hi! I say, can you fly?"

"I never tried," said Tom. "Why?"

"Because, if you can, I would advise you to say nothing to the old lady about it. There, take a hint. Goodbye."

Away Tom went for seven days and seven nights due northwest, till he saw the last of the gairfowl, standing up on the Allalonestone, all alone. She was a very grand old lady, full three feet high and bolt upright, like some old Highland ruler. She had on a black velvet gown and a white apron, and she had a very high bridge to her nose (which is a sure mark of high breeding), and a large pair of white spectacles on it, which made her look rather odd; but it was the ancient fashion of her house.

And, instead of wings, she had two little feathery arms with which she fanned herself as she complained of the dreadful heat.

Tom came up to her very humbly and made a bow, and the first thing she said was:

"Have you wings? Can you fly?"

"Oh, dear, no, ma'am. I would not think of such a thing," said cunning little Tom.

"Then I shall have great pleasure in talking to you, my dear. It is refreshing nowadays to see something without wings. They must all have wings, forsooth, now, every new upstart sort of bird, and fly. What can they want with flying, and raising themselves above their proper station in life? In the days of my ancestors no birds ever thought of having wings, and did very well without; and now they all laugh at me because I keep to the good old fashion. Why, the very marrocks and dovekies have wings, the vulgar creatures, though they are poor little things; and so do my own cousins, the razorbills, who are gentlefolk and ought to know better than to try and ape their inferiors."

So she went running on while Tom tried to get a word in. At last he did, when the old lady got out of breath and began fanning himself again. Then he asked if she could tell him the way to Shiny Wall.

"Shiny Wall? Who should know better than I? We all came from Shiny Wall, thousands of years ago, when it was decently cold, and the climate was fit for gentlefolk. You must go, my little dear, you must go . . . let me see, I am sure, that is, really, my poor old brains are getting quite rattled. Do you know, my little dear, I am afraid you must ask some of these vulgar birds if you want to know for I have totally forgotten."

And the poor old gairfowl began to cry tears of pure oil, and Tom was quite sorry for her. But he was sorry for himself too, for he was at his wits' end whom to ask.

But then there came a flock of petrels, who are Mother Carey's own chickens, and Tom fell in love with them at once, and called to them to ask the way to Shiny Wall.

"Shiny Wall? Do you want Shiny Wall? Then come with us and we will show you. We are Mother Carey's own chickens, and she sends us out over all the seas to show the good birds the way home."

Tom was delighted, and swam off to them.

Now Tom was all agog to start for Shiny Wall, but the petrels said no. They must go first to Allfowlsness and wait there for the great gathering of all the seabirds before they start for their summer breeding places far away in the Northern Isles. There they would be sure to find some birds going to Shiny Wall; but he must promise never to tell where Allfowlsness was, lest men go there and shoot the birds, and stuff them, and put them into town museums instead of leaving them to play, and feed, and breed, and work in Mother Carey's water garden, where they ought to be.

So where Allfowlsness is nobody must know, and all that is to be said about it is that Tom waited there many days.

After a while, the birds began to gather at Allfowlsness in thousands and tens of thousands, darkening all the air: swans and black-necked geese, harlequins and eiders, harelds and garganeys, smews and goosanders, divers and loons, grebes and dovekies, auks and razorbills, gannets and petrels, skuas and terns, and gulls beyond all naming or numbering. And they paddled and washed and splashed and combed and brushed themselves on the sand till the shore was white with feathers. And they quacked and clucked and gabbled and chattered and screamed and whooped as they talked over matters with their friends, and settled where they would go to breed that summer, till you might have heard them ten miles off.

Then the petrels asked this bird and that whether they would take Tom to Shiny Wall. But one group was going to Sutherland, and one to the Shetlands, and one to Norway, and one to Spitzbergen, and one to Iceland, and one to Greenland, and none were going to Shiny Wall. So, instead, the good-natured petrels said that they would show him part of the way themselves but they were only going as far as Jan Mayen's Land and after that, he would have to take care of himself.

Then all the birds rose up and streamed away in long black lines, north, and northeast, and north west, across the bright, blue summer sky; and their cry was like ten thousand packs of hounds and ten thousand peals of bells. Only the puffins stayed behind, and killed the young rabbits and laid their eggs in the rabbit burrows, which was a harsh practice, certainly; but a man must see to his own family.

Then, as Tom and the petrels went northeastly, it began to blow right hard. But Tom and the petrels didn't care, for the gale was behind them, so away they went over the crests of the billows, as merry as so many flying fish.

And at last they saw an ugly sight: the blackened side of a large ship, waterlogged in the trough of the sea. Its funnel and masts were overboard and swayed and surged under the lee; its decks were swept as clean as a barn floor, and there seemed to be no living soul on board.

The petrels flew up to the ship and wailed round it,

for they were very sorry, but they expected to find some salt pork; and Tom scrambled on board and looked all round him, frightened and sad.

And there, in a little bed lashed tight under the bulwark, lay a baby fast asleep: the very same baby, Tom saw at once, which he had seen in the singing lady's arms.

He went up to it and wanted to wake it, but out jumped from under the bed a little black-and-tan terrier dog, which began barking and snapping at Tom, and would not let him touch the bed.

Tom knew the dog's teeth could not hurt him, but at least it could shove him away, and did; and he and the dog fought and struggled, for he wanted to help the baby and did not want to throw the loyal dog overboard. But as they were struggling, there came a tall, green sea, and walked in over the weather side of the ship, and swept them all into the arms of the waiting waves.

"Oh, the baby, the baby!" screamed Tom. But the next moment he did not scream at all, for he saw the little bed settling down through the green water, with the baby in it, smiling and fast asleep. And he saw the fairies come up from below, and carry baby and cradle gently down in their soft arms; and then he knew it was all right, and that there would be a new water-baby in St. Brandan's Isle.

And the poor little dog?

Why, after he had kicked and coughed a little, he sneezed so hard that he sneezed himself right out of his skin and turned into a water-dog, and jumped and danced round Tom, and ran over the crests of the waves, and snapped at the jellyfish and the mackerel, and followed Tom the whole way to the Other-end-of-Nowhere.

So they went on again, till they caught sight of the peak of Jan Mayen's Land, standing up like a white sugarloaf, two miles above the clouds.

And there they fell in with a whole flock of molly-mocks, who were feeding on a dead whale.

"These are the birds to show you the way," said Mother Carey's chickens. "We cannot help you farther north. We don't like to get among the ice pack for fear it would nip our toes: but the mollies dare fly anywhere."

So the petrels called to the mollies, but they were so busy and greedy, gobbling and pecking and spluttering and fighting over the blubber, that they did not take the least notice.

"Come, come," said the petrels, "you lazy, greedy lubbers. This young gentleman is going to Mother Carey, and if you don't go with him to help, you

Tom was frightened at the idea of a schoolmistress, but she was a beautiful little girl (page 175)

He began crying and screaming for Mrs. Bedonebyasyoudid
(page 184)

Onto the quarter-deck came a very pretty lady with a baby in her arms (page 189)

He saw the little bed settling down through the water, with the smiling baby in it (page 197)

won't earn your discharge from her, you know."

"Greedy we are," said a great fat old molly, "but lazy we ain't; and, as for lubbers, we're no more lubbers than you. Let's have a look at the lad."

And he flapped right into Tom's face, and stared at him in the most impudent way (for the mollies are audacious, as all whalers know), and then asked him where he hailed from, and what land he sighted last on this voyage.

And when Tom told him, he seemed pleased, and said he was a good plucky boy to have managed to get so far.

"Come along, lads," he said to the rest, "and give this little chap a leg over the ice pack for Mother Carey's sake. We've eaten blubber enough for today, and we'll even work out a bit of our time by helping the lad."

So the mollies took Tom up on their backs and flew off with him, laughing and joking; and oh, how they did smell of train oil!

"Who are you, you jolly birds?" asked Tom.

"We are the spirits of the old Greenland skippers (as every sailor knows), who hunted right whales and horse whales many hundreds of years ago. But, because we were saucy and greedy, we were all turned into mollies, to eat whale's blubber all our days. But lubbers we are not, and could sail a ship now against anyone in the North Sea, though we don't hold with this new-fangled steam. And it's a shame for those black imps of petrels to call us so; but because they're her grace's pets, they think they may say anything they like."

And now they came to the edge of the ice pack, and beyond it they could see Shiny Wall looming through mist and snow and storm. But the pack rolled horribly upon the swell, and the ice giants fought and roared, and leapt upon each other's backs, and ground each other to powder, so that Tom was afraid to venture among them in case he should be ground to powder too. And he was the more afraid when he saw lying among the ice pack the wrecks of many a gallant ship, some with masts and yards all standing, some with the seamen frozen fast on board. Alas, alas, for them! They were all true English hearts, and they came to their end like good knights errant in search of the white gate that never was opened yet to their search.

But the good mollies took Tom and his dog up, and flew with them safe over the pack and the roaring ice giants, and set them down at the foot of Shiny Wall.

"And where is the gate?" asked Tom.

"There is no gate," said the mollies.

"No gate?" cried Tom, aghast.

"None. Never a crack of one, and that's the whole of the secret, lad, as better fellows than you have found to their cost; and if there had been, by now they'd have killed every right whale that swims the sea."

"What am I to do then?"

"Dive under the floe, to be sure, if you have pluck."

"I've not come so far to turn back now," said Tom, "so here goes for a header."

"A lucky voyage to you, lad," said the mollies. "We knew you were one of the right sort. So goodbye."

"Why don't you come too?" asked Tom.

But the mollies only wailed sadly. "We can't go yet, we can't go yet," and flew away over the ice pack.

So Tom dived under the great white gate which never was opened yet, and went on in black darkness at the bottom of the sea for seven days and seven nights. And yet he was not a bit frightened. Why should he be? There was nothing to fear. He was a brave English lad, whose business it is to go out and see all the world.

And at last he saw the light, and clear, clear water overhead; and up he came a thousand fathoms among clouds of sea moths, which fluttered round his head. The dog snapped at them till his jaws were tired, but Tom hardly noticed them at all, he was so eager to get to the top of the water and see the pool where the good whales go.

And a very large pool it was, miles and miles across, though the air was so clear that the ice cliffs on the opposite side looked as if they were close at hand. All round it the ice cliffs rose in walls and spires and battlements, and caves, and bridges, and galleries in which the ice fairies live, whose work it is to drive away the raging storms and clouds so that Mother Carey's pool may lie calm from year's end to year's end.

The sun acted as police and walked round outside every day, peeping just over the top of the ice wall to see that all went right; and now and then it played magic tricks or had an exhibition of fireworks to amuse the ice fairies. For it would make itself into four or five suns at once, or paint the sky with rings and crosses and crescents of white fire and stick itself in the middle of them and wink at the fairies; and I daresay they were very much amused, for anything's fun in lonely places.

And there the good whales lay, the happy, sleepy beasts, upon the still, oily sea. They were all right whales, you must know, and finners, and razorbacks, and bottlenoses, and spotted sea unicorns with long, ivory horns.

They were quite safe and happy there, and all they had to do was to wait quietly in Peacepool till Mother Carey sent for them to make them into new beasts out of old.

Tom swam up to the nearest whale and asked the way to Mother Carey.

"There she sits in the middle," said the whale.

Tom looked, but all he could see in the middle of the pool was one peaked iceberg, and he said so.

"That's Mother Carey," said the whale, "as you will find when you get to her. There she sits making old beasts into new ones all the year round."

"How does she do that?"

"That's her concern, not mine," said the old whale.

"I suppose," said Tom, "she cuts up a great whale like you into a whole shoal of porpoises?"

At which the old whale laughed violently, and Tom went on to the iceberg, wondering.

When he came near it, it took the form of the grandest old lady he had ever seen: a white marble lady, sitting on a white marble throne. And from the foot of the throne there swam away, out and out into the sea, millions of newborn creatures, of more shapes and shades than anyone ever dreamed. And they were Mother Carey's children, whom she makes out of the seawater all day long.

Like some grown people who ought to know better, he expected to find her

snipping,
piecing,
fitting,
stitching,
cobbling,
basting,
filing,
planing,
hammering,
turning,
polishing,
shaping,
measuring and so forth, as people do when they work at making something.

But, instead of that, she sat quite still with her chin upon her hand, looking down into the sea with two great, grand blue eyes, as blue as the sea itself. Her hair was as white as the snow, for she was very, very old, in fact, as old as anything which you are likely to come across, except for the difference between right and wrong.

And, when she saw Tom, she looked at him very kindly.

"What do you want, my little man? It is a long time since I saw a water-baby here."

Tom told her his errand, and asked the way to the Other-end-of-Nowhere.

"You ought to know yourself, for you have been there already."

"Have I, ma'am? I'm sure I cannot remember anything about it."

"Then look at me."

And, as Tom looked into her large blue eyes, he recollected the way perfectly.

Now, was not that strange?

"Thank you, ma'am," said Tom. "Now I won't trouble your ladyship any more. I hear you are very busy."

"I am never busier than I am now," she said, without stirring a finger.

"I heard, ma'am, that you were always making new beasts out of old."

"So people think. But I am not going to trouble

myself to make things, my little dear. I sit here and make them make themselves."

But people do not yet believe that Mother Carey is as clever as all that, and they will not believe it till they too go the journey to the Other-end-of-Nowhere.

"And now, my pretty little man," said Mother Carey, "you are sure you know the way to the Other-end-of-Nowhere?"

Tom thought and found that he had forgotten it completely.

"That is because you took your eyes off me."

Tom looked at her again and remembered. Then he looked away and forgot in an instant.

"But what am I to do, ma'am? For I can't keep looking at you when I am somewhere else."

"You must do without me, as most people have to do, for nine hundred and ninety-nine thousandths of their lives, and look at the dog instead; for he knows the way well enough, and will not forget it. You may meet some very queer-tempered people there, who will not let you pass without this passport of mine, which you must hang round your neck and take care of; and, of course, as the dog will always go behind you, you will find you have to go the whole way backward.

"Backward!" cried Tom. "Then I shall not be able to see my way."

"On the contrary, if you look forward, you will not see a step before you and be certain to go wrong. But, if you look behind you and watch carefully whatever you have passed, and especially keep your eye on the dog, who goes by instinct and therefore can't go wrong, then you will know what is coming next, as plainly as if you saw it in a looking glass."

Tom was very much astonished, but he obeyed her, for he had learned always to believe what the fairies told him.

"So it is, my dear child," said Mother Carey; "and I will tell you a story, which will show you that I am perfectly right, as it is my custom to be.

"Once upon a time, there were two brothers. One was called Prometheus because he always looked before him. He boasted that he was, therefore, wise beforehand. The other was called Epimetheus because he always looked behind him. He did not boast at all, but said humbly and without airs, that he would rather prophesy after the event.

"Well, Prometheus was a very clever fellow, of course, and invented all sorts of wonderful things. But, unfortunately, when anyone tried to use them, they would not work at all, and so very little has come of them and his hard work went unrewarded.

"But Epimetheus, who was a very slow fellow, indeed, was known among people as a clod and a muff and a milksop and a sleepy head, and an oaf and a simpleton and so forth. And he did very little for many years; but what he did, he never had to do over again.

"And what happened in the end? There came to the two brothers the most beautiful creature that ever was seen, Pandora by name, which means 'all the gifts of the gods.' But because she had a strange box in her hand, the fanciful, forecasting, suspicious, prudential, theoretical, deductive, prophesying Prometheus, who was always settling what was going to happen, would have nothing to do with pretty Pandora and her box.

"But Epimetheus took her and it, as he took everything that came, and married her for better or for worse, as every man ought whenever he has even the chance of a good wife. And they opened the box between them, of course, to see what was inside. Otherwise, of what possible use could it have been to them?

"And out flew all the ills which flesh is heir to, all the children of the four great bogeys of Self-will, Ignorance, Fear, and Dirt, for instance:

Measles,
Scarlatina,
Idols,
Whooping cough,
Wars,
Famines,
Quacks,
Unpaid Bills,
Tight Stays,
Bad Wine,
Despots,
Demagogues,
And, worst of all,
Naughty Boys and Girls.

But one thing remained at the bottom of the box, and that was Hope.

"So Epimetheus got a great deal of trouble, as most men do in this world. But he got the three best things in the world into the bargain: a good wife, and experience, and hope. Meanwhile, Prometheus had just as much trouble, and a great deal more (as you will hear) of his own making and with nothing to make up for it but wild ideas spun from his own brain, as spiders spin webs from their stomach.

"And Prometheus kept on looking before him, so far ahead that, as he was running with a box of matches (which were the only useful things he ever invented, and do as much harm as good), he trod on his own nose, and tumbled down (as most deductive philosophers do), whereby he set the Thames on fire; and they have hardly yet put it out. So he had to be chained to the top of the mountain, with a vulture to give him a peck whenever he stirred, so that he would not turn the whole world upside down with his prophecies and his theories.

"But stupid old Epimetheus went on working and grubbing, with the help of his wife Pandora, always looking behind him to see what had happened, till he really learned now and then what would happen next; and understood so well on which side his bread was buttered, and which way the cat jumped, that he began to make things which would work, and go on working too: to make things to till and drain the ground, and looms, and ships, and railroads, and steam ploughs, and electric telegraphs, and to foretell famine and bad weather.

"And his children are the scientists, who get good, lasting work done in the world; but the children of Prometheus are the fanatics, and the theorists, and the bigots, and the bores, and the noisy, windy people, who tell silly folk what will happen, instead of looking to see what has happened already."

Now, was not Mother Carey's a wonderful story? And, I am happy to say, Tom believed every word of it.

For it happened to Tom as she said. Though he was very sorely tired, by keeping the dog to heels (or rather to toes, for he had to walk backward), he could see pretty well which way the dog was hunting. Even so, it was much slower work to go backward than to go forward.

I am proud to say that Tom never turned his head round once, all the way from Peacepool to the Other-end-of-Nowhere. He kept his eye on the dog, and let him pick out the scent, hot or cold, straight or crooked, wet or dry, up hill or down dale, by which means he never made a single mistake, and saw all the wonderful and hitherto by-no-mortal-man-imagined things, which it is my duty to relate to you in the next chapter.

CHAPTER EIGHT

MR. GRIMES AGAIN

Now, as soon as Tom had left Peacepool, he came to the white lap of the great sea mother, ten thousand fathoms deep. There she makes world-dough all day long for the steam giants to knead, and the fire giants to bake, till it has risen and hardened into mountain loaves and island cakes.

And there Tom was very near being kneaded up in the dough and turned into a fossil water-baby, which would have astonished the Geological Society of New Zealand some hundreds of thousands of years later.

For, as he walked along in the silence of the sea twilight on the soft white ocean floor, he was aware of a hissing, and a roaring, and a thumping, and a pumping, like all the steam engines in the world going at once. And when he came near, the water grew boiling hot. Not that that hurt him in the least, but it also grew as horrible as gruel; and every moment he stumbled over dead shells, and fish, and sharks, and seals, and whales, which had been killed by the hot water.

And at last he came to the great sea serpent itself, lying dead at the bottom; and as it was too wide to scramble over, Tom had to walk round it three-quarters of a mile and more, which put him greatly out of his way. Then, when he had made it round, he came to the place called Stop. And there he stopped, and just in time.

For he was on the edge of a vast hole in the bottom of the sea, and clear steam was rushing and roaring up it, enough to work all the engines in the world at once, and so clear that it was bright as light at moments; and Tom could see up almost to the top of the water above, and down below into the pit for nobody knows how far.

But, as soon as he bent his head over the edge, he got such a rap on the nose from pebbles that he jumped back again. For, as the steam rushed up, it rasped away the sides of the hole and hurled it up in the sea in a shower of mud and gravel and ashes; and then it spread all around, and sank again, and covered in the dead fish so fast that, before Tom had stood there five minutes, he was buried in silt to his ankles, and began to be afraid that he would actually

There came to the two brothers the beautiful Pandora, which means "All the gifts of the gods" (page 212)

He got such a rap on the nose from pebbles that he jumped back again (page 218)

be buried alive if he didn't think of a way out.

And perhaps he would have been except that, while he was thinking, the whole piece of ground on which he stood was torn off and blown upward, and away flew Tom a mile up through the sea, wondering what was coming next.

At last he stopped, thump! Then he found himself held tight between the legs of the most amazing bogey he had ever seen.

It had I don't know how many wings, as big as the sails of a windmill, and spread out in a ring like them; and with them it hovered over the steam which rushed up, as a ball hovers over the top of a fountain. And for every wing above it had a leg below, with a claw like a comb at the tip, and a nostril at the root; and in the middle it had no stomach and one eye; and as for its mouth, that was all on one side, like the madreporian tubercle in a starfish is. Well, it was a very strange beast, but no stranger than some dozens which you may see.

"What do you want here," it cried peevishly, "getting in my way?" And it tried to drop Tom, but he held on tight to its claws, thinking himself safer where he was.

So Tom told him who he was, and what his errand was. And the thing winked its one eye, and sneered:

"I am too old to be taken in in that way. You have come after gold, I know you have."

"Gold! What is gold?" asked Tom, who really did not know; but the suspicious old bogey would not believe him.

After a while, Tom began to understand a little. For, as the vapours came up out of the hole, the bogey smelled them with his nostrils, and combed them and sorted them with his combs; and then, when they steamed up through them against his wings, they were changed into showers and streams of metal.

From one wing fell gold dust, and from another silver, and from another copper, and from another tin, and from another lead, and so on, and sank into the soft mud, into veins and cracks, and hardened there. That is how it comes to pass that the rocks are full of metal.

But all of a sudden, somebody shut off the steam below, and the hole was left empty in an instant. Then down rushed the water into the hole, in such a whirlpool that the bogey spun round and round as fast as a top. But that was all in his day's work, and he paid no attention to it. So all he did was to say to Tom:

"Now is your time, youngster, to get down if you

are in earnest, which I don't believe."

"You'll soon see," said Tom; and away he went, as bold as Baron Munchausen, and shot down the rushing cataract like a salmon on the way to a breeding ground.

When he got to the bottom, he swam till he was washed on the shore of the Other-end-of-Nowhere; and to his surprise, he found it as most other people do, much more like This end-of-Somewhere than he had been in the habit of expecting. Indeed, some parts reminded Tom of his life on land.

And first he went through Wastepaper-land, where all the stupid books lie in heaps, up hill and down dale, like leaves in winter in a forest. There he saw people digging and grubbing among them, to make worse books out of bad ones, and threshing chaff to save the dust of it; and they did a big business too, especially among children and people who knew no better.

Then he went by the sea of slops, to the mountain of messes and the territory of snacks, where the ground was very sticky, for it was made entirely of bad toffee and was full of deep cracks and holes choked with fallen fruit, and green gooseberries, and sloes, and crabs, and whinberries, and hips and haws, and all the nasty things which little children will try to eat, if they can get them.

But the fairies hide them out of the way in that country as fast as they can, and very hard work they have, and of very little use it is. For as fast as they hide away the old trash, foolish and wicked people make fresh trash full of lime and poisonous paints, and actually go and steal recipes out of old Madame Science's big book to invent poisons for little children, and sell them at markets and fairs and stores. Very well. Let them go on.

Your mother and father and teachers cannot catch them, though they are setting traps for them all day long. But the fairy with the birch rod will catch them all in time, and make them begin at one corner of their shops, and eat their way all the way through and out at the other end, by which time they will have such stomach aches that they will be cured of poisoning little children.

Then Tom came to the Island of Polupragmosyne. There everyone pokes into the business of the people who live near them, and a very noisy place it is, as might be expected, considering that all the inhabitants act like representatives to the "Parliament of Mankind and the Federation of the World." So they are always twisting their mouths, and crying that the fairies' grapes are sour.

There Tom saw:
ploughs drawing horses,
nails driving hammers,
birds' nests stealing boys,
books writing authors,
bulls keeping china shops,
monkeys shaving cats,
dead dogs drilling live lions,
the ill-educated as principals of
colleges, actors not in the least
out of place as popular preachers. In short, everyone set to do something which they had not learned, because in what they had learned, or pretended to learn, they had failed.

There stands the Pantheon of the great Unsuccessful, from the builders of the Tower of Babel and the leaning Tower of Pisa to politicians who lecture on the constitutions which are not put into effect, conspirators on the revolutions which ought to have suceeded, economists on the schemes which ought to have made everyone's fortune, inventors on the discoveries which ought to have "set the world on fire."

When he got into the middle of the town, they all talked at once to tell him his way; or rather, to show him that he did not know his way; for, as for asking him what way he wanted to go, no one ever thought of that.

But one pulled him this way and another pushed him that way, and a third cried:

"You musn't go west, I tell you. It is destruction to go west."

"But I am not going west, as you may see," said Tom.

And another, "The east lies here, my dear. I assure you this is the east."

"But I don't want to go east," said Tom.

"Well, then, at all events, whichever way you are going, you are going wrong," they all cried with one voice, and this was the only thing which they ever agreed about. And all pointed at once to all the thirty-two points of the compass, till Tom thought all the signposts in England had come together and fallen into fighting.

Whether he would ever have escaped from the town it is hard to say, if the dog had not taken it into his head that they were going to pull his master to pieces, and tackled them so sharply about the gastrocnemius muscle, that he gave them some business of their own to think about; and while they were rubbing their bitten calves, Tom and the dog got away safely.

On the borders of that island he found Gotham, where the sages live, the same who dragged the pond because the moon had fallen into it, and planted a hedge around the cuckoo to keep spring all the year. He found them bricking up the town gate because it was so wide that little folk could not get through. So he went on, for it was no business of his, only he could not help saying that in his country, if the kitten could not get in at the same hole as the cat, she could stay outside and mew.

Then Tom came to the great land of Hearsay, in which there are no less than thirty odd kings, besides half a dozen republics, and perhaps more by the next mail.

And there he fell into a deep, dark, deadly, and destructive war, waged by the princes and potentates of those parts, both spiritual and temporal, against, what do you think?

One thing I am sure of. That unless I told you, you would never guess. Nor would you know how they waged that war either, for all their strategy and military art consisted of the safe and easy process of holding their ears and screaming, "Oh, don't tell us!" and then running away.

And running after them, both day and night, came a very poor, lean, seedy, hard-worked old giant.

He was made up principally of fish bones and parchment, put together with wire and Canada balsam, and smelled strongly of spirits, though he never drank anything but water; but he used spirits somehow, there was no denying.

He had a huge pair of spectacles on his nose, a butterfly net in one hand, and a geological hammer in the other; and he was hung all over with pockets full of collecting boxes, bottles, microscopes, telescopes, barometers, ordnance maps, scalpels, forceps, photographic apparatus, and all the other equipment for finding out everything about everything, and a little more too. And, strangest of all, he was running not forward but backward, as fast as he could.

All the good folk ran away from him, except for Tom, who stood his ground and dodged between his legs; and the giant, when he had passed him, looked down and cried, as if he was most pleased and comforted:

"What? Who are you? And you actually don't run away like all the rest?" But he had to take his spectacles off, Tom noticed, in order to see him plainly.

Tom told him who he was, and the giant pulled out a bottle and a cork instantly, to collect him with.

But Tom was too sharp for that, and dodged between his legs and in front of him, and then the giant could not see him at all.

"No, no, no!" said Tom, "I've not been round the world, and through the world, and up to Mother Carey's haven, beside being caught in a net and called a holothurian and a cephalopod, to be bottled up by an old giant like you."

And when the giant understood what a great wanderer Tom had been, he made a truce with him at once, and would have kept him there to this day to pick his brains, so delighted was he to find someone to tell him what he did not know before.

"Ah, you lucky little dog!" said he at last, quite simply, for he was the simplest, pleasantest, honest, kindliest old scholar of a giant that ever turned the world upside down without intending it. "Ah, you lucky little dog! If only I had been where you have been, and had seen what you have seen!"

"But why do you run after all these poor people?" asked Tom, who liked the giant very much.

"My dear, it's they who have been running after me, father and son, mother and daughter, for hundreds and hundreds of years, throwing stones at me till they have knocked off my spectacles fifty times, though they can't catch me, for every time I go over the same ground, I go faster and grow bigger. All I want is to be friends with them and tell them something to their advantage, only somehow they are strangely afraid of hearing it. But I suppose I am not sophisticated or wise enough and have no tact."

"But why don't you turn round and tell them so?"

"Because I can't. You see, I am one of the sons of Epimetheus, and must go backward if I am to go at all."

And on went the giant, behind-before, like a bull in a china shop, till he ran into the steeple of the great idol temple (for they are idolaters in those parts, of course, or else they would never be afraid of giants), and knocked the upper half right off, hurting himself horribly in the small of the back.

And down he sat on the nave of the temple, not knowing much about temples. Whereon, as was to be expected, the roof caved in bodily, smashing the idols and sending the priests flying out of doors and windows like rabbits out of a burrow when a ferret goes into it.

But he didn't notice, for out of the dust flew a bat, and the giant had him in a moment.

"Dear me! This is most important! Here is a cognate species to that which Macgilliwaukie Brown insists is confined to the Buddhist temples of Little

Tibet; and now that I look at it, I think it may only be a variety produced by a certain difference of climate!"

And having bagged his bat, up he got and on he went while all the people ran off, being in a pretty bad mood over having their temple smashed before their very eyes.

"Well," thought Tom, "this is an interesting quarrel, with a good deal to be said on both sides. But it is no business of mine."

Then Tom came to a very famous island, which in the days of the great globe trotter, Captain Gulliver, was called the Isle of Laputa. But Mrs. Bedonebyasyoudid has renamed it the Isle of Tomtoddies, all heads and no bodies.

And when Tom came near it, he heard such a grumbling and grunting and growling and wailing and weeping and whining that he thought people must be shearing little lambs, or cropping puppies' ears, or drowning kittens; but when he came nearer still, he began to hear words among the noise, which was the Tomtoddies' song that they sing morning and evening, and all night too, to their great idol Examination:

"I can't learn my lesson. The examiner's coming!"

And that was the only song which they knew.

And when Tom got on shore, the first thing he saw was a great pillar on one side of which was inscribed, "Playthings are not allowed here." He was so shocked at this that he would not stay to see what was written on the other side. Then he looked round for the people of the island; but instead of men, women, and children, he found nothing but turnips and radishes and beets, without a single green leaf among them, and half of them burst and decayed, with toadstools growing out of them. Those which were left began crying to Tom, in half a dozen different languages at once, and all of them badly spoken, "I can't learn my lesson; do come and help me!" And one cried, "Can you show me how to extract this square root?"

And another, "Can you tell me the distance between Lyra and Camelorpardalis?"

And another, "What is the latitude and longitude of Scappoose in the northwest of Oregon, U.S.A.?

And so on, and so on, and so on, till one would have thought they were all trying for entrance into university or law school.

"And what good on earth will it do if I did tell you?" asked Tom.

Well, they didn't know that. All they knew was

that the examiner was coming.

Then Tom stumbled on the hugest and softest nimblecomequick turnip you ever saw, filling a hole in a crop of beets, and it cried to him, "Can you tell me anything at all about anything you like?"

"About what?" says Tom.

"About anything you like; for as fast as I learn things, I forget them again. So my mamma says that my intellect is not adapted for methodic science, and says that I must go in for general information."

Tom told him that he did not know general information, nor any officers in the army, though he once had a friend that became a drummer boy. But he could tell him a great many strange things which he had seen in his travels.

So Tom told him nicely, while the poor turnip listened very carefully; and the more he listened, the more he forgot, and the more he forgot the more water ran out of him.

Tom thought he was crying, but it was only his poor brains running away from being worked so hard; and as Tom talked, the unhappy turnip streamed juice all over itself, and split, and shrank till nothing was left on him but rind and water. At this, Tom ran away in a fright, for he thought he might be arrested for killing the poor turnip.

Tom was so puzzled and frightened with all he saw that he was longing to ask the meaning of it; and at last he stumbled over a respectable old stick lying half covered with earth. It was a very stout and worthy stick, for it had once belonged to Roger Ascham, the famous scholar. On its head was carved a scene depicting King Edward the Sixth with the Bible in his hand.

"You see," said the stick, "these were once as pretty little children as you could wish to see, and might have been so still if they had only been left to grow up like human beings, and then handed over to me. But their foolish fathers and mothers, instead of letting them pick flowers, and make mudpies, and find birds' nests, and dance round the gooseberry bush, as little children should, kept them always at lessons, working, working, working, learning week-day lessons all week days, and Sunday lessons all Sunday, and weekly examinations every Saturday, and monthly examinations every month, and yearly examinations every year, everything seven times over, as if once was not enough, and enough as good as a feast, till their brains grew big and their bodies grew small, and they were all changed into turnips, with hardly anything but water inside; and still their foolish parents actually pick the leaves off as fast as they grow, so they won't have anything green about them."

"Ah!" said Tom, "If dear Mrs. Doasyouwouldbedoneby knew of it, she would send them a lot of tops, and balls, and marbles, and ninepins, and make them all as happy as larks."

Then he came to a very quiet place called Leaveheavenalone. And there the sun was drawing water out of the sea to make steam threads, and the wind was twisting them to make cloud patterns, till they had between them made the loveliest wedding veil of Chantilly lace, and hung it up in their own Crystal Palace for anyone who could afford to buy it. The good old sea didn't mind, for she knew they would pay her back honestly. So the sun span, and the wind wove, and all went well with the great steam loom.

And at last, after innumerable adventures, each more wonderful than the last, Tom saw before him a huge building, much bigger, and, what is most surprising, a great deal uglier than a new lunatic asylum, though it was not built quite of the same materials. No. The walls of this building were built on an entirely different principle, which need not be described here now because it has not yet been discovered.

Tom walked toward this great building, wondering what it was and having the strange idea that he might find Mr. Grimes inside, till he saw three or four people running toward him and shouting "Stop!" When they came nearer, they were nothing else but police truncheons, running along without legs or arms.

Tom was not astonished. He was long past being surprised.

So he stopped, and when the first truncheon came up and asked his business, he showed Mother Carey's pass; and the truncheon looked at it in the oddest fashion, for it had one eye in the middle of its upper end so that when it looked at anything, being quite stiff, it had to slope itself, and poke itself till it was a wonder why it did not tumble over. However, as it was full of the spirit of justice, as all police in the world and their truncheons ought to be, it was always in a position of stable equilibrium, whichever way it put itself.

"All right. Pass on," it said at last. And then it added: "I had better go with you, young man." And Tom had no objection, for such company was both respectable and safe. So the truncheon coiled its thong neatly round its handle to prevent itself tripping, for the thong had become loose in running,

The more he listened, the more he forgot, and the more water ran out of him (page 233)

A wicket in the door opened, and out looked a tremendous old blunderbuss (page 239)

and marched on by Tom's side.

"Why have you no police to carry you?" asked Tom after a while.

"Because we are not like those clumsily made truncheons in the land-world, which cannot go without having a whole person to carry them about. We do our own work for ourselves, and do it very well, though I say so myself."

"Then why have you a thong to your handle?" asked Tom.

"To hang ourselves up by when we are off duty of course."

Tom had his answer, and had no more to say till they came up to the large iron door of the prison. And there the truncheon knocked twice, with its own head.

A wicket in the door opened and out looked a tremendous old brass blunderbuss, charged up to the muzzle with slugs, who was the doorkeeper. Tom couldn't help but start back a little at the sight of him.

"What case is this?" asked the doorkeeper in a deep voice out of his broad, bell mouth.

"If you please, sir, it is no case, only a young gentleman from her ladyship, who wants to see Grimes, the master sweep."

"Grimes?" said the blunderbuss. And he pulled in his muzzle, perhaps to look over his prison lists.

"Grimes is up chimney number 345," he said from inside. "So the young gentleman had better go onto the roof."

Tom looked up at the enormous wall, which seemed at least ninety miles high, and wondered how he would ever get up; but, when he hinted that to the truncheon, it settled the matter in a moment. For it whisked round, and gave him such a shove behind that it sent him up to the roof in no time, with his little dog under his arm.

And there he walked along the tiles, till he met another truncheon, and told it his errand.

"Very good," it said. "Come along; but it will be of no use. He is the most unremorseful, hard-hearted, foul-mouthed fellow I have in charge and thinks about nothing but beer and pipes, which are not allowed here, of course."

And at last they came to chimney number 345. Out of the top of it, his head and shoulders just showing, stuck Mr. Grimes, so sooty, and bleary, and ugly that Tom could hardly bear to look at him. And in his mouth was a pipe which was not lit; though he was pulling at it with all his might.

"Attention, Mr. Grimes," said the truncheon.

"Here is a gentleman to see you."

But Mr. Grimes only said bad words and kept grumbling, "My pipe won't draw. My pipe won't draw."

"Keep a civil tongue and pay attention!" said the truncheon, and popped up just like Punch, hitting Grimes such a crack over the head with itself that his brains rattled inside like a dried walnut in its shell. He tried to get his hands out and rub the place, but he could not, for they were stuck fast in the chimney. Now he was forced to listen.

"Hey!" he said, "why, it's Tom! I suppose you have come here to laugh at me, you spiteful little atomy?"

Tom assured him he had not, and only wanted to help him.

"I don't want anything except beer and a light for this bothering pipe, and I can't get either one in this terrible place."

"I'll get you one," said Tom, and he picked up a live coal (there were plenty lying about) and put it to Grimes' pipe; but it went out instantly.

"It's no use," said the truncheon, leaning itself up against the chimney and looking on. "I tell you, it is no use. His heart is so cold that it freezes everything that comes near him. You will see that soon, and you will understand plain enough."

"Oh, of course, it's my fault. Everything's always my fault," said Grimes. "Now don't hit me again" (for the truncheon stood very straight and looked very wicked). "You know you would not dare to hit me if my arms were only free."

"But can't I help you in any other way? Can't I help you to get out of this chimney?" asked dear little Tom.

"No," interposed the truncheon. "He has come to the place where everybody must help themselves, and he will find that out, I hope, before I am done with him."

"Oh, yes," said Grimes, "of course it's me. Did I ask to be brought to this prison? Did I ask to be made to sweep your foul chimneys? Did I ask to have lighted straw put under me to make me go up? Did I ask to stick fast in the very first chimney of all, because it was so shamefully clogged up with soot? Did I ask to stay here, I don't know how long, a hundred years, I do believe, and never get my pipe, or my beer, or anything at all fit for a beast, let alone a man?"

"No," answered a solemn voice behind. "Nor did Tom when you behaved to him in the very same way."

It was Mrs. Bedonebyasyoudid. And, when the truncheon saw her, it stood bolt upright at attention, and made such a low bow that, if it had not been full of the spirit of justice, it would have tumbled on its end, and probably hurt its one eye. Tom made his bow too.

"Oh, ma'am," he said, "don't think about me. That's all past and gone just as good times and bad times and all times pass. But may not I help poor Mr. Grimes? May I try to get some of these bricks away so that he can move his arms?"

"You may try, of course," she said.

So Tom pulled and tugged at the bricks, but he could not move one. And then he tried to wipe Mr. Grimes' face, but the soot would not come off.

"Oh, dear!" he said. "I have come all this way, through all these terrible places, to help you, and now I am of no use after all."

"You had best leave me alone," said Grimes. "You are a good natured, forgiving little chap, and that's the truth; but you'd best be off. The hail's coming on soon, and it will beat the eyes out of your little head."

"What hail?"

"Why, hail that falls here, every evening, and till it comes close to me, it's like so much warm rain; but then it turns to hail over my head and knocks me around like small pebbles."

"That hail will never come any more," said the fairy. "I have told you before what it was. It was your mother's tears, those which she shed when she prayed for you on her knees. But your cold heart froze it into hail. Now she is in heaven, and will no longer shed tears for her graceless son."

Then Grimes was silent awhile; and then he looked very sad.

"So my old mother's gone, and I was not there to speak to her! Ah! a good woman she was, and might have been a happy one in her little school there in Vendale, if it hadn't been for me and my bad and wicked ways."

"Did she keep the school in Vendale?" asked Tom. And then he told Grimes the whole story of his going to her house, and how she could not bear the sight of a chimney sweep, and then how kind she was, and how he turned into a water-baby.

"Ah!" said Grimes, "she had good reason to hate the sight of a chimney sweep. I ran away from her and took up with the sweeps, and never let her know where I was, or sent her a penny to help her, and now it's too late, too late!" said Mr. Grimes.

And he began crying and blubbering like a big baby, his mouth twisted into a pout and his pipe dropped out of his mouth and broke to bits.

"Oh, dear, if I was but a little chap in Vendale again, to see the clear beck, and the apple orchard, and the yew hedge, how different I would be! But it's too late now. So you go along, you kind little chap, and don't stand looking at a man crying who's old enough to be your father, and never feared the face of man, or of worse either. But I'm beat now, and beat I must be. I've made my bed and I must lie on it. Foul I would be, and foul I am, as an Irishwoman said to me once, and little I heeded it. It's all my own fault, but it's too late." And he cried so bitterly that Tom began crying along with him.

"Never too late," said the fairy, in such a strange, soft, new voice that Tom looked up at her; and she was so beautiful for the moment that Tom half fancied she was her sister.

Nor was it too late. For, as poor Grimes cried and blubbered, his tears did what his mother's could not do, and Tom's could not do, and nobody's on earth could do for him; for they washed the soot off his face and off his clothes, and then they washed the mortar away from between the bricks, and then the chimney crumbled down, and Grimes began to crawl out of the rubble.

Up jumped the truncheon, ready to hit him a

tremendous thump on the crown and so drive him down again like a cork into a bottle. But the fairy stopped it.

"Will you obey me if I give you a chance?"

"As you please, ma'am. You're stronger than me, that I know too well, and wiser than me, that I also know too well. And, as for being my own master, I've fared badly enough with that so far. So order me to do whatever your ladyship pleases, for I'm beat, and that's the truth."

"Be it so. Then you may come out. But remember, disobey me again, and you go into a still worse place."

"I beg your pardon, ma'am, but I never disobeyed you that I know of. I never had the pleasure of setting eyes on you till I was brought to these ugly quarters."

"Never saw me? Who said to you, 'Those that will be foul, foul they will be'?"

Grimes looked up, and Tom looked up too; for the voice was that of the Irishwoman who met them the day they went to Harthover together. "I gave you your warning then, but you gave it to yourself a thousand times before and since. Every bad word that you said; every cruel and mean thing that you did; every time that you got tipsy; every day that you went dirty; you were disobeying me, whether you knew it or not."

"If I'd only known ma'am . . . "

"You knew well enough that you were disobeying something, though you did not know it was me. But come out and take your chance. Perhaps it may be your last."

So Grimes stepped out of the chimney, and really, if it had not been for the scars on his face, he looked as clean and respectable as a master sweep need look.

"Take him away," said she to the truncheon, "and give him his ticket-of-leave."

"And what is he to do, ma'am?"

"Get him to sweep out the crater of Mount Etna. He will find some very steady men working out their time there, who will teach him his business; but mind, if that crater gets choked again, and there is an earthquake in consequence, bring them all to me, and I shall investigate the case with great care and the utmost detail."

So the truncheon marched Mr. Grimes off, who looked as meek as a drowned worm.

And for all I know or do not know, he is sweeping the crater of Etna to this very day.

"And now," said the fairy to Tom, "your work here is done. You may as well go back to your home."

"I would be very glad to go," said Tom, "but how am I to get up that great hole again, now that the steam has stopped blowing?"

"I will take you up the backstairs, but I must bandage your eyes first, for I never allow anybody to see those backstairs of mine."

"I am sure I would not tell anybody about them, ma'am, if you tell me not to."

"Aha! So you think, my little man. But you would soon forget your promise if you got back into the land-world. So come. Now I must bandage your eyes." So she tied the bandage on his eyes with one hand, and took it off with the other hand.

"Now," she said, "you are safe up the stairs." Tom opened his eyes very wide, and his mouth too. For he felt as though he had not moved a single step. But, when he looked round him, there could be no doubt that he was safe up the backstairs, wherever they may be.

The first thing which Tom saw was the black cedars, high and sharp against the rosy dawn, and St. Brandan's Isle reflected double in the still, broad, silver sea. The wind sang softly in the cedars, and the water sang among the caves. The sea birds sang as they streamed out into the ocean, and the land birds as they built nests among the boughs; and the air was so full of song that it stirred St. Brandan and his hermits as they slumbered in the shade; and they moved their good old lips, and sang their morning hymn amid their dreams. But among all the voices, one came across the water sweeter and clearer, for it was the voice of a young woman.

And as Tom neared the island, there on a rock sat the most graceful creature that ever was seen, looking down with a dreamy expression on her face, her chin on her hand and paddling in the water with her feet. And when they came to her, she looked up, and, of course, it was Ellie.

"Oh, Ellie," said Tom. "How much you have grown!"

"Oh, Tom. How you have grown too!"

And no wonder. They were both quite grown up: he into a tall man and she into a beautiful woman.

"I guess I should be grown," she said. "I have had time enough, for I have been sitting here waiting for you for hundreds of years, till I thought you were never coming."

"Hundreds of years," thought Tom. But he had seen so much in his travels that he had given up being astonished by anything; and, indeed, he could think of nothing but Ellie. So he looked at Ellie, and Ellie looked at him, and they both liked the employment so much that they stood and looked for seven years more.

At last they heard the fairy say, "Attention, Tom and Ellie. Are you never going to look at me again?"

"We have been looking at you all this while," they said, for they thought they had been.

"Then look at me once more," said she.

They looked, and both of them cried out as one, "Oh, who are you?"

"You must be our dear fairy Mrs. Doasyouwouldbedoneby."

"No, you are good Mrs. Bedonebyasyoudid, but you have become beautiful now!"

"To you," said the fairy. "But look once more, my dears."

"You are Mother Carey," said Tom in a very low, solemn voice, for he had found out something which made him very happy, and at the same time frightened him more than all that he had seen.

"But you are young again."

"To you," said the fairy. "Look again."

"You are the Irishwoman who met me the day I went to Harthover!"

And when they looked, she was none of them and yet all of them at once.

"My name is written in my eyes, if you have eyes

to see it there."

And they looked into her big, deep, soft eyes, and they changed again and again into every hue, as the light changes in a diamond.

"Now read my name," said she at last.

And her eyes flashed clear, white, blazing light for a moment. But the children could not read her name, for they were dazzled and hid their faces in their hands.

"Not yet, young things, not yet," said she, smiling; and then she turned to Ellie.

"You may now take him home with you on Sundays, Ellie. He has won his spurs in the great battle of life, and is fit to go with you and be a man because he has done the thing he did not like."

So Tom went home with Ellie on Sundays, and sometimes on week days too; and he is now a great man of science, and can plan railroads, and steam engines, and electric telegraphs, and photography, and many more things. And all this from what he learned when he was a water-baby, way underneath the sea.

"And, of course, Tom married Ellie?"

My dear child, what a silly notion! Don't you know that no one ever marries in a fairy tale, except a prince or a princess?

"And Tom's dog?"

Oh, you may see him any clear night in July, for the old dog-star was so worn out by the last three hot summers that there have been no dog days since. So they had to take him down and put Tom's dog up in his place. Therefore, as new brooms sweep clean, we may hope for some warm weather this year. And that is the end of my story.

EPILOGUE

And now, my dear friends, what should we learn from this story?

We should learn thirty-seven or thirty-nine things, I am not exactly sure which: but one thing, at least, we may learn and that is this – when we see efts in the pond, never to throw stones at them or put them into aquariums with sticklebacks so that the sticklebacks make them jump out of the glass and into somebody's workbox, and so come to a bad end. For these efts are nothing else but the water-babies who are lazy and dirty and will not learn their lessons and keep themselves clean. And what happens is that their skulls grow fat, their jaws grow out, and their brains grow small, and their tails grow long, and they lose all their ribs, and they never get into the clear rivers, but hang about in dirty ponds, and live in the mud, and eat worms, as they deserve to do.

But that is no reason to ill-treat them. You should pity them and be kind to them and hope that one day they will wake up and try to improve, and become something better once more.

For, perhaps if they do, then after 379,423 years, nine months, thirteen days, two hours and twenty-one minutes, their brains may grow bigger, and their jaws may grow smaller, and their tails may whither off, and they will turn into water-babies again, and perhaps after that, into land-babies, and after that into men or women.

You know they won't, of course. Well, I daresay you know best. But some people are very fond of those poor little efts for they never did anybody any harm: their only fault is that they do no good. And, what with dangers from ducks, pike, sticklebacks, and water-beetles, it is a wonder how they survive. But some folks can't help hoping that they never have another chance somehow, somewhere.

Meanwhile, do learn your lessons and be grateful that you have plenty of water to wash in. And remember, as I told you at first, that this is a fairy tale, and only fun and pretence. Therefore, you are not to believe a word of it – even if it is true.

Out of the top stuck Mr. Grimes, so ugly that Tom could hardly bear to look at him (page 240)

And in the twinkling of an eye, there stood Ellie, smiling and looking happy (page 186)